'What happened next, Bianca?'

'His hands were up my skirt, digging into my buttocks, inside my panties. I could feel how urgent he was, how desperate.'

Her eyes were closed and she could hear once more the sound of the rain on the roof of the shed, smell the must and the lust, feel the boy's whole body quaking as if in fear. She licked her lips.

'Go on, Bianca,' said the Doctor. 'What happened?'

'He broke away without warning and I wondered what was wrong, what had I done? But he turned me round so that I faced the doorway and he lifted my skirts again and pulled my panties down around my thighs . . .'

Also available from Headline

The Lusts of the Borgias
Love Italian Style
Ecstasy Italian Style
Rapture Italian Style
Amorous Liaisons
Lustful Liaisons
My Duty, My Desire
Bare Necessities
Saucy Habits
Eroticon Dreams
Eroticon Desires
Play Time
Carnal Days
Carnal Nights
Hot Type
The Sensual Mirror
French Frolics
Claudine
Wild Abandon
Fondle in Flagrante
After Hours
French Thrill
In The Mood
A Slave to Love
Kiss of Death
Amorous Appetites
The Blue Lantern
Sex and Mrs Saxon

Bianca

Maria Caprio

HEADLINE

First published in 1993
by HEADLINE BOOK PUBLISHING PLC

10 9 8 7 6 5 4 3 2

ISBN 0 7472 3981 9

Printed and bound in Great Britain by
HarperCollins Manufacturing, Glasgow
Typeset by CBS Felixstowe Suffolk

HEADLINE BOOK PUBLISHING PLC
Headline House
79 Great Titchfield Street
London W1P 7FN

Bianca

Chapter 1

Rome

Bianca talked too much and drank too much during dinner because she was nervous. She smiled and laughed too easily, and touched his hand to indicate an intimacy she didn't feel. He was understanding and did his best to help her relax.

Robert was a good man, a sensitive man. He was also handsome, his hair touched with grey at the temples, successful in business and divorced three years. The divorce had not been of his making and he had not rushed into relationships since. He was not a flirt, he was thirty-eight years old, and, to many women, he was the perfect catch.

The same could be said about Bianca.

She was beautiful, with wide brown eyes and black hair, independently wealthy after the death of her husband, and thirty years old.

They talked about the inconsequential and about life and he was an attentive listener.

She said: 'I don't accept many invitations for dinner.'

'I don't offer many.'

'I know. That's why I said yes.'

'You mean it wasn't my devastating good looks?'

He said it with a smile to indicate it was a joke.

'Your looks helped. Being eligible didn't.'

'Am I eligible?'

'Yes.'

She said it without guile.

'I suppose I am.' He lit a cigarette. 'But the way

you talk about it makes having dinner sound like a meeting to discuss a merger.'

Bianca forced a smile; she didn't want her reply to be misconstrued.

'In a way it could be.'

'You're a very direct woman, Bianca.'

'I always have been. My husband encouraged it.'

'Do you still miss him?'

'Very much. Do you miss your wife?'

'Not at all. The divorce was a relief after the lies and the arguments and the lawyers.' He gave her a wry smile. 'It left me emotionally marooned. I saw a psychiatrist for six months.'

'Did he help?'

'I don't know. Maybe it needed six months anyway, for the memories to fade.'

'I don't want my memories to fade.'

'If they're good ones, they won't.' His smile became warm and he touched her hand. 'You really were happy, weren't you?'

'Yes.'

'It's time you were happy again.'

For this very special evening she had taken a suite in the hotel where they dined and, after they had finished, he escorted her upstairs.

When the lift doors closed they were totally alone for the first time and the beat of her heart increased. But this was not passion, it was the onset of panic. She stood motionless and stared straight ahead, afraid in case Robert touched her. He didn't.

The ping of the lift bell announced their arrival at the correct floor and she started with shock at the sound. The doors opened and they stepped out and walked along the corridor. He held out his hand and she gave him the key.

He opened the door, stepped inside to switch on a light and came out again. He smiled and she realised she couldn't stand in the corridor all night.

Her voice cracked when she spoke.

'Would you like to come in?'

How, she wondered, would he interpret her voice?

They went inside and he closed the door. She walked through the lighted lobby into a sitting room that was still dark, self-conscious of the way her limbs moved, of how she looked, of the silk of her dress.

If he only knew what she was wearing beneath the dress then maybe, maybe . . .

Bianca turned to face him, resting her buttocks against the back of a sofa, holding the tensions in check. Her handbag fell from her hand and slid onto the cushions behind her.

Robert smiled gently. He didn't switch on any more lights and he walked towards her. She bit the inside of her lip and breathed in short gasps through her nostrils.

He said: 'Don't say anything. There's no need to say anything.'

His hands were gentle in her hair, a finger traced her cheekbone to her chin which he turned upwards so that he could kiss her softly on the mouth. She gulped and her lips resisted when his tongue attempted to part them. He kissed her neck, and her ear, his tongue flickering wetly on her skin, and he made shushing noises of comfort as his body pressed against her and his hands moved around her.

Bianca began to shake imperceptibly.

This was wrong. It was foolish. Why should she feel this way?

She moved her head and found his mouth with hers and made herself open her lips and push with her tongue.

His body moved against her and she could feel the size of him and the heat of him against her stomach. One hand was in the small of her back and moving down over her buttocks. His fingers were digging into the softness and pulling her against his hardness. He was pushing open her legs with his knee.

Bianca broke her mouth free. Her hands were still resting on the back of the sofa and she gripped it for support. She was losing her breath as the panic rose . . . and then the tensions went as she fainted.

She was unconscious only for seconds. When she came round, she kept her eyes half-closed as protection against having to deal with the situation.

Her body had slumped backwards over the sofa and Robert had lowered her gently onto its cushions. The manoeuvre had caused her legs to splay open and her skirt to rise around her thighs, leaving her stockinged legs naked to his gaze. Something hard was sticking into her and she caught her breath until she realised it was her handbag.

Robert was kneeling by the side of the sofa, unaware she was conscious, looking at her legs and up the skirt into the shadows, touching the flesh above the silk of the stocking with fingers so gentle they could have been a dream.

If he wanted to, he could take her now and she would be powerless to stop him and powerless to blame him. After all, she had invited him here and offered encouragement.

He could take her now!

He didn't. He straightened her legs and pulled down the skirt, stroked her face and whispered her name.

She stopped pretending and began to cry.

Robert was the perfect gentleman as well as the perfect catch. He asked if she wanted to talk, if there was anything he could do, but she shook her head and eventually he said goodnight, kissed her on the forehead and left.

She went into the bedroom, the tensions replaced

by despair, and looked at herself in the full-length mirror. The tears had smudged her make-up but she was still undeniably beautiful. She pulled the zipper at the back and let the dress slide off to pool around her feet and exchanged a sad stare with the woman who stood there in high heels and underwear made for sex.

Yet she had been unable to do it, even in the neutral surroundings of a hotel room and with a perfect gentleman. She turned out the light and lay on the bed and her fingers touched herself and she imagined they were the fingers of a stranger and other tensions mixed in with the despair.

Tomorrow she would get help. It had been four years since Michel had died. Tomorrow she would get help.

Chapter 2

Paris

Cosmo was forty-five but looked older, was bald and overweight, and lived with the permanent stress of a nagging wife and three spoiled daughters.

He was a bloated, lesser version of Bianca's late husband; an elder brother by eight years who had always lived in the shadow of the younger. Michel had been more intelligent, witty, compassionate and successful with women.

The brothers had been born in France but, in adulthood, had lived in different cities in different countries, each looking after a different sphere of the family business. Cosmo had stayed in Paris while Michel had moved to Rome. Both brothers were linguists but the rest of Cosmo's family did not speak Bianca's native language of Italian and Bianca did not speak French.

On the occasions Bianca had visited, she had been grateful for the attentiveness and kindness of the older brother in a country where she was rendered deaf and dumb by her inability to communicate.

Bianca had no close family of her own, and had relinquished friendships since the death of her husband. Besides, the help she needed now could not be given by a friend. The only person she felt she could talk to was Cosmo.

He was a relative and yet distant; he had been warm and understanding in the past, and he was her husband's brother.

She telephoned him the next morning and, the day

after, she took an Alitalia flight from Rome to Paris.

The journey was an escape from failure and an entry into the unknown. She wore slacks to deny her sexuality and, from leaving the aircraft, did not understand a word anyone said to her.

She was marooned, surrounded by natives whose customs she might unwittingly offend, attempting to gauge meaning from inflections and raised eyes. The experience frightened and stimulated her, as if the aeroplane journey had been the start of another kind of journey.

Bianca took a taxi to the company's city premises, which occupied the fourth floor in a tower block, handing the driver the address on a piece of paper and offering him a choice of banknotes when they arrived.

When she was finally shown into Cosmo's office by a secretary, she felt she had completed the first part of a challenge.

They sat in black leather armchairs and faced each other across a black marble coffee table upon which the secretary placed cups and a pot of coffee. After the formalities of greetings, they lapsed into a tentative silence.

Cosmo looked more bloated than the last time she had seen him, but there was still a hint of her late husband there, and there was concern in his eyes.

'What is your problem, Bianca? You know I will do anything I can to help.'

'It's not easy to explain. But I have to tell somebody and there is only you I can tell.'

'Anything I can do. You know that.'

A small silence.

Bianca said: 'It's four years since . . .'

He nodded.

'I know. It was terrible, but time heals, Bianca. You have to let it heal.'

'I want it to. And the hurt has healed. I want more than anything to be normal again, but I can't.'

'You are a beautiful woman. You have wealth. You have no material problems. What can be wrong?'

She expelled breath, a sigh of sorrow.

'My problem is sexual. Since . . . for four years I have been unable to have a relationship with a man.'

A long silence.

She looked up, hopefully, at his face. Having made her confession, she would be grateful simply for it to be accepted, let alone to receive aid, comfort and direction.

Cosmo sat back and crossed his legs. He was biting on his lower lip. He shook his head.

'You poor child. I had no idea.'

She smiled at him for the sympathy. Her secret had been hers for four years and she felt relief that she had shared it.

'I don't know what to do,' she said.

Cosmo coughed politely into his hand.

'When you say . . . relationship. You mean an actual . . . sexual . . . relationship?'

'Yes. I can be comfortable with a man as long as I know there is no possibility of sexual contact. When that possibility arises, I begin to panic. I cannot help myself. I panic, I faint, I cause a scene.'

'Perhaps you haven't met the right man?'

'It's not that.'

'Perhaps you're living with a ghost?'

'I'm living with a memory, but not a ghost.'

Cosmo put the palms of his hands flat together as if in prayer and put the tips of his fingers against his lips.

Another silence, but she felt at ease; a little excited perhaps at revealing her ache after so long, but comfortable in his presence.

'Has this happened often?'

'No. Not often, because it will take someone special to replace what I have lost. There have not been that many men who have attracted me. But there have been some.'

'When was the first time?'

'Three years ago. It took a year for me to begin to notice men again.'

'And since then?'

'I thought that maybe the first time, the chemistry had been wrong. That I froze because there was something about him that I didn't like. Something indefinable. I met someone else two or three months later and it happened again. After that, I wondered whether it was me. The panic began with that suspicion. I tried five or six more times, but every time was a failure and a humiliation. I tried again, two nights ago, and realised I needed help.'

'What sort of help, Bianca?'

'I don't know. Some kind of counselling perhaps - a psychiatrist? I thought you might know someone, might be able to find out where I should go, who I should see?'

'You really believe you need help?'

The emotions she had held in check began to surface and tears pricked her eyes.

'I want to be a woman again, Cosmo. A complete woman. I want to be able to love again.'

Another silence, this time of stretched hope.

He said: 'Let me make some enquiries. Don't worry. I'll find someone to help.'

Bianca wanted to remain anonymous and took a room at a hotel rather than stay at Cosmo's home outside the city.

The hotel was large, one of a chain that circled the world, all identical and clinical. It was as if the hotels were run for their own sake on a self-perpetuating cycle of consumerism: refurbishment, food and drink replenishment, staff recruitment, and guest enrolment. The guests, and everybody and everything else, were there to serve the needs of the hotel, rather than the other way round.

Bianca recognised the cycle and the need and felt comfortable to be part of it.

She remained in her room, except to have lunch with Cosmo the next day. The day after that, he visited her at the hotel.

'I have found someone,' he said.

The relief made her smile.

'He is a sexual therapist, a prominent man in his field, but radical in his approach. You may not like him or his methods.'

'You say he is good?'

'His reputation is excellent.'

'Then I must see him.'

Cosmo allowed the silence to grow while they looked into each other's eyes. He was again kissing his fingers in prayer.

'There are conditions, even before you make your first visit.'

'What conditions?'

'When you came to my office two days ago, you were wearing trousers. You wore trousers yesterday and are wearing them again today.'

She looked puzzled. The slacks she wore were expensive and elegant.

'So?'

'The Doctor was specific when he asked me about you. He asked how you were dressed and I told him. He says that to be cured of sexual repression, you must rid yourself of sexual defences. He says trousers are sexual defences.'

She knew what he meant.

'Tell me the condition?'

'The Doctor says you must be feminine. You must dress as if you were meeting a man for a sexual assignation. Your clothes must reflect the sexuality you are trying to deny. I've seen the way you used to dress. Beautifully, exquisitely. You must do so again, otherwise he won't see you.'

She nodded slowly. The logic was obvious; besides, she *had* been wearing trousers to deny her sexuality.

'Alright.'

'Bianca, are you sure?'

'I'm sure. When can I see him?'

'This afternoon. I'll take you there myself.'

Chapter 3

Bianca wore a blue silk dress, matching silk underwear, tan stockings and high-heeled shoes. As a first course in the treatment, it made her feel good to have the summer breeze circulating between her legs.

Cosmo said: 'You look beautiful.'

They went in a taxi to a large house in the suburbs that was protected by high walls and an iron gate. Cosmo paid the driver, spoke into an electronic box that was attached to the wall, and the gate clicked open. They crossed a courtyard that was fringed by young trees in blossom, and climbed three steps to the front door that opened as they arrived before it.

A taciturn young man in a dark suit indicated where they should go, and Cosmo led Bianca across a tiled floor, past a sweeping staircase, to an open door.

'Doctor?'

'Come in, come in.'

They entered a room that was lined with bookshelves and large mirrors, and which contained armchairs, a desk and a consultant's couch.

The Doctor was a small elderly man, with a full head of white hair. He wore glasses, a three-piece suit and a bow tie. Cosmo made the introductions and the Doctor shook Bianca's hand with a firm, moist grip and gave her a confident smile.

He said to her brother-in-law: 'I think it would be better if you left Bianca and myself alone.'

He had spoken in Italian for Bianca's sake, and she sensed he was fluent in the language.

Cosmo looked at Bianca and she nodded to him that she was happy to be left alone.

'I'll be outside,' he said.

He left and closed the door behind him and the Doctor indicated a chair. Bianca sat. He leant against his desk, folded his arms and gazed at her benignly.

'Cosmo has given me the outline of your problem, and I want to say right now that you have already crossed the most significant barrier to a return to normality: you have admitted the problem to yourself and you have confided in those who can help.'

He sat in an armchair that faced Bianca.

'Your husband died four years ago?'

'Yes.'

'And since then you have not been able to enjoy a fulfilling relationship with a man?'

'That is correct.'

'Let us be specific. Since your husband died, have you had sexual intercourse with a man?'

'On one occasion.'

'And?'

'It was an unhappy experience.'

'Have you had an emotional relationship with a man?'

'No. I don't allow them to develop because I know they will lead to a physical relationship. On the occasions they have reached the start of a physical relationship, I have been unable to consummate it.'

The Doctor nodded.

'You gave a great deal to your husband?'

'We gave a great deal to each other.'

'And when he died, he took with him part of what you gave him.'

'Perhaps.'

'Your relationship with your husband was deep. The loss you felt when he died was equally deep. The blockage you have created with your body and emotions is a protection. You are reluctant to give again, in case you lose it again.'

'Perhaps.'

'Don't worry. It is not uncommon and there is treatment. However, my methods are sometimes judged extreme, even though they work.' He paused. 'They work, that is, if you have total confidence in what we are doing and a real desire to shed the inhibitions that are making you less than complete.'

She nodded, both nervous at what his methods might be, and hopeful at what they might achieve.

'First, we shall talk. And naturally, we shall talk about sex, for sex is the great motivator of life and no-one should be ashamed of the feelings it arouses. Freud said sex is the basic impulse in all animals. Man happens to be a complicated animal and sometimes his sexual desires and problems are complicated.

'Remember, everybody is obsessed with sex, whether it is a nun who denies her sex for God, or a nymphomaniac who enjoys the physical release so much she cannot get enough. Whether it is a husband who boasts of his prowess, or a wife who complains of the lack of attention she is being paid.

'Sex drives men and women to success in business, to ecstasy in union. Animals copulate to populate but people copulate for pleasure.'

He smiled at his slogan before he continued.

'Within these walls, nothing else matters but honesty. Hopes, experiences, hidden desires, they should all be revealed. I have studied sex since puberty and nothing can shock me. My own first sexual encounter happened when I was eight years old.'

He raised his eyebrows and nodded.

'My parents employed a young woman to look after me while they were at business. She enjoyed taking me to bed and cuddling me naked. Of course I didn't understand straight away what she was doing, but I soon began to enjoy it.' He grinned. 'I was annoyed when my mother found out and sacked the girl.'

Bianca smiled in response, finding it difficult to imagine the Doctor naked at any age and in the arms of a woman.

'And now, my dear.' He got up and pointed to the couch. 'If you would be so kind as to make yourself comfortable, we'll begin.'

She got to her feet and self-consciously sat upon the couch before lifting up her legs, holding her skirt close to her thighs and stretching out, her head and shoulders resting on the slanted support.

He smiled and looked down at her.

'Comfortable?'

'Yes.'

'Good.'

He sat in a chair near her feet and she could no longer see him. All she could see was a cream ceiling with cracked plaster that shaped the continents of an unknown world. It was as if she had levitated from reality.

His voice: 'Now, Bianca. Relax. Let your body sink into the couch. Let the tensions drain away.'

He paused and her breathing settled.

'You're completely safe, you're completely relaxed. Find the clouds on the ceiling. Big, white fluffy clouds of summer. They're your clouds, Bianca. Soft and friendly. They're taking you back. Back to when you were a girl. To those summers long ago. Do you see the clouds, Bianca?'

She saw them. She floated with them.

'Ride them, Bianca. Ride the clouds back to when you were a girl. To when you were sixteen. You are sixteen, Bianca. You have boyfriends, you go on dates, you kiss and pet.'

Yes, she did.

'Give me a memory of a boy, an encounter. The

first memory in your mind. Now.'

'We were in a park. It was raining. We sheltered in a wooden hut.'

She was surprised to hear her own voice, and surprised at the depth of her memory. She could smell the damp.

'What happened in the hut?'

'We kissed. He pushed against me. He touched me . . . no, he felt me.'

She remembered it vividly.

'How did you feel?'

'Excited. Shaky. My mouth was dry. He was big in his trousers. He pushed it . . .'

He allowed a short silence.

'Go on, Bianca.'

'I was leaning with my back against the door jamb. My shoulders were against it but I pushed my hips out. My legs were open and he had a thigh between them, pushing it against me. I could feel the thing in his trousers hard against my leg.'

'The thing in his trousers?'

'Yes. The thing . . .'

'What's it called, Bianca? Give it a name. What thing, Bianca?'

'His prick. His prick was big in his trousers and he was breathing heavily. We had started kissing but he wasn't kissing anymore, he was covering my mouth with his as if to stop me from saying no.'

'Did you want to say no?'

'No. I was excited. I wasn't in control. I felt . . .'

More silence.

'Find the word, Bianca. How did you feel?'

'I felt horny. I'd never felt like that before. My hips were moving against his thigh. He was rubbing his thing, his prick, against me and I was rubbing myself against him.'

Her eyes were closed and she could hear the rain

through the open door of the shed, smell the must and the lust, feel his whole body quaking as if in fear.

'What happened, Bianca? What happened next?'

'His hands were up my skirt, digging into my buttocks, inside my panties. I could feel how urgent he was, how desperate.' She licked her lips. 'Then he broke away, suddenly, without warning, and I wondered what was wrong, what I had done? But he turned me round so that I faced the door jamb, and he lifted my skirts again and pushed himself against me. I was confused and he'd taken away his thigh that I had been pushing against.'

Bianca remembered she had tried to push herself against the door jamb, to find relief against the hard wood but he hadn't let her.

'Go on, Bianca. What happened?'

'He pushed my panties down around my thighs and his hands gripped my flesh and went between my legs. He pushed a finger inside me but he was rough and didn't know what he was doing and it hurt and I made a noise of pain and he stopped. My eyes were closed and I didn't know what was happening but he was manoeuvring behind me and then I felt him, his hard thing, his prick, released from his trousers and hot against my bottom. He held my hips and rubbed his prick against my bottom.

'I was shocked and opened my eyes. I couldn't understand how it had gone this far. Then he parted my legs with his knee and pushed his thing, his prick, between my thighs. I was frightened he might go inside me and excited at the same time.'

'Did he go inside you, Bianca?'

'No. He held my hips and thrust against my bottom and he came between my legs.'

The Doctor allowed the silence.

Bianca's eyes were still closed and her lips still moved. She hadn't finished.

He waited.

'Go on, Bianca.'

'While he was doing it, while he was between my legs from behind, a gardener was watching us.'

She fell silent.

'Where was the gardener?'

'He was sheltering from the rain by a fence. The hut was in a rose garden. It was where the gardeners went to drink their wine and coffee. He must have been coming back there when he saw us.'

'How long had he been there?'

'I don't know. I saw him when I opened my eyes, when I felt the boy's prick push against me. I watched him and he watched us until the boy came between my legs.'

'What happened then?'

'We ran away. The gardener shouted at us to stop but we ran away.'

The rain had been cool on her face, cool on her frustrations.

'Did you do anything else with the boy?'

'No, I never went out with him again. We didn't speak after we ran away. We stopped in some bushes and I wiped his sperm from the front of my thighs with a handkerchief. He wanted to start again when he saw me do that, but I wouldn't. At the gates, we went different ways.'

But she kept the handkerchief.

This time, the Doctor let the silence settle.

Bianca kept her eyes closed, remembering the feelings rather than the details, wanting to touch herself, trying not to move her hips against the material of the knickers between her legs as she lay on the couch.

'You were sixteen when this happened?'

'Yes.'

'How old was the boy?'

'Sixteen or seventeen, about the same age.'

'Did you have a regular boyfriend at that time?'

'There was one boy. A year older than me. We went together for about six months. We split up because I wouldn't let him go all the way.'

'But you went part of the way?'

'Yes.'

'Do you have a memory of him?'

'Not really.'

'Oh come, Bianca. You must have memories of him. If you went together for six months, you must have been doing things on a regular basis. Were you doing things on a regular basis?'

'Yes.'

'What sort of things?'

'The usual sort of things.'

'The memories you have of this boy are not good memories, are they?'

'No.'

'Why?'

'He used me. Showed me off. He liked his friends to know he had power over me.'

'How? Tell me how, Bianca? Give me an example.'

'Sometimes we went to his house. He had his own apartment over the garage. The house and garage were built into the side of a small hill. The window at the rear of the apartment was only about six feet above the lawn at the back of the house.

'One afternoon we were in his room. It was summer and the window was open. We had been doing what he normally liked to do. He had taken his trousers off and he had taken my panties off. I always kept my dress on because my breasts were not big, but I let him take my panties off as long as he promised not to go all the way. I think he only kept his promise because he didn't know how to go all the way.

He had been rubbing it against my stomach and

my bottom and between my legs. He normally came quickly and then did it again. But this afternoon he didn't. Then three of his friends called for him. They went on the lawn and shouted at the window. He went to the window and talked to them. Then he called me to say hello to them, so I went to the window and looked down at them. From where they were, they could only see us from the waist up.

'They made lewd remarks about having a good time, and he pushed against me from behind as if to cuddle me, and I had to hold myself against the window sill. Then, while he was still talking to his friends, he pulled up my skirt and pushed his prick between my legs.

'I couldn't move and I couldn't protest. My face was red and he kept talking to them, saying he wouldn't be long, and he pushed it in and out between my legs.'

A tremor of anger, shame and arousal ran through Bianca as she lay on the couch. She had never felt him so hard or so hot.

The Doctor said: 'What happened?'

'He came against my bottom. Then he put his trousers on and went to join his friends.'

She remembered the lust and longing in the faces of the three boys outside, dry-mouthed and nervous with butterfly stomachs. She had closed the window, drawn the curtains and wiped herself and wondered why she was shaking so much.

Bianca was shaking again, now, on the couch, one leg rising so that her inner thighs rubbed together. She wondered if the Doctor had noticed.

The Doctor said: 'Were there other occasions?'

'Yes.'

'Tell me about them.'

'There were many occasions that I wasn't aware of until afterwards.'

'Such as?'

She licked her lips and remembered the smell of grass and the land in the summer.

'He often took me into the fields. We would lie down in a secluded place and he would do things. I was always nervous in case anyone walked by and saw us or was watching us, but he said we were alone. Afterwards, I realised there were times when we were not alone.'

'What do you mean?'

'I know that on occasions he arranged for his friends to hide in a certain place before we got there. Then they watched while he did things to me.'

'How did you know this?'

'I became suspicious because he behaved differently on those occasions when his friends were watching. He was more dominant, rougher, as if he was playing a role. Then, once, as he made me change position, I saw a movement in the bushes nearby and knew I was right. Afterwards, when we met up with his friends, they would smirk and make jokes among themselves and look at my body.'

'What did you do?'

'What do you mean?'

'Did you stop your boyfriend's intimacies? Did you tell him you knew you were being watched?'

'No.'

'Why not?'

Why had she let him continue? Why had she gone to the secret place again when she knew the same arrangements had been made and allowed it all to happen?

'Why, Bianca?'

'Because it excited me.'

'Being watched was exciting?'

'Yes. I didn't realise that was my reason at the time. I told myself I had no choice, that I should do as my boyfriend wished. And while it happened I remained nervous, with fantasies of them all leaving their hiding places and joining us. But afterwards, when I was alone, the excitement filled me.

'Did you masturbate?'

The question was casual; the term was functionary. The memories had filled her with languid sexuality and she now felt a small thrill of excitement, like a fingertip brushing her clitoris, at telling an elderly man that she masturbated.

'Yes,' she said. 'When I was alone, I masturbated.'

'Does the thought of the boyfriend excite you now?'

'Not the boyfriend – the situation. That still excites me.'

'Tell me about one of the occasions.'

'There were so many occasions.'

'Tell me about one of the last times you went to your secret place. When you knew you were being watched. Tell me what you were wearing, tell me every detail.'

It had been a Sunday afternoon. Mass in the dark echoing church had been purgatory. During it, she had remembered the other occasions and wondered if he would again take her to the place that afternoon. The itch between her legs had been deliciously sinful.

'I wore a blue cotton dress; a shift dress with no waistline. It was short and ended above the knee. The day was hot and beneath it I wore only panties.' She smiled to herself. 'White cotton panties. I also wore white ankle-socks and sandals.'

At the time, she had been embarrassed at the traditional way in which she was expected to dress, particularly on Sundays, and her boyfriend had also been displeased that she did not look more mature. Later, she had realised the potency of wearing such simple clothes with their intimation of innocence. She had frequently dressed like that for Michel.

'I went to meet my boyfriend and saw him talking to his three friends. When they saw me approaching, they rode off on their bicycles. I knew then he had been making the arrangements with them.

'We went to our usual place, through long grass and then down a slope towards a copse of trees. We had flattened an area of the grass near the trees with our bodies. On those occasions when we really would be alone, he would hold my hand as we walked there. He was never really capable of tenderness or romance at that time, but I assumed that he thought it necessary to try and show affection. When we were to have an audience, he didn't hold my hand but led me there without speaking, as if I were a chattel.

'There were no preliminaries when we lay down. He pushed me on my back and kissed me, forcing his tongue into my mouth, as if claiming a right. His hands felt my body through the dress, only briefly touching my breasts which were still small.

'He was never interested in my breasts, simply interested in what was between my legs and what was between his legs. He was never really interested in me; I just happened to be available and female, a girl upon whom to experiment and use until he was able to get a woman.

'He pulled the dress up to my waist and I raised my hips to help him but when he attempted to pull down my panties I resisted. It was my way of telling him he was going too quickly and he usually responded by kissing me some more. It was a pretence and a set of responses we followed. But this time he didn't respond; he knocked my hands away and pulled off the panties completely, something I had never allowed before when we had been outside.

'There was a change in him. He had always been a bully but now I saw he could also be a rapist. He unfastened his trousers and pushed them down his thighs. His erection was already big and he lay on me, holding my arms outspread, and opened my legs with his knees. He grunted and heaved against me, his prick moving haphazardly between my legs, sometimes rubbing against my buttocks, sometimes along my vagina and against my clitoris. When that happened, it sparked a thrill that I didn't understand. He had never thrilled me before. Only the situation had thrilled me when I thought about it afterwards.'

Bianca remembered those times afterwards. When she was alone in her room and how she had recalled the fear and the tensions and the way his hands shook as if he was no longer in control of himself. And how her own fingers had gone between her legs and brought her intense orgasms, one after the other after the other.

The Doctor said: 'Did he penetrate you, Bianca?'

'No. He didn't penetrate me. The only lubrication was from him, my body provided none. But to his friends it looked as if he was inside me, which was what he wanted them to believe, and if they believed it, it was almost as good as if he had done it.

'After a while, he knelt up and pushed my head down towards his prick. This, again, was a departure from what he normally did. I knew what he wanted me to do but I didn't know how to do it. If I had known, I would have fellated him. Because I didn't, he got angry.

'He wiped the end of his prick across my face, leaving wet trails on my skin, and the smell from it was very strong. I had never seen it this close before and I was amazed at how it appeared to be bloated, the head purple and the vein throbbing.

'Somehow he got it in my mouth but the taste was alien and the size frightened me; I thought I might choke. It was only in my mouth for two or three seconds before I pulled away, but that was enough to make him come. He held it in his right hand and directed his sperm into my face.

'There was a lot and I watched, partly frightened, partly excited, partly fascinated, as it discharged. It went on my cheek, my chin, my mouth and into my hair. As he came he made a lot of noise; he groaned and shouted obscenities. From the woods I thought I heard someone else groaning, too, as if they had orgasmed at the sight.

'Afterwards, I pushed my skirt down and lay on my back, not knowing what to do about the sperm on my face. I tasted what was on my lips and didn't like it. It was cold and salty. He lay alongside me and when he had regained his breath, he looked at my face and began to spread the sperm with his fingers, rubbing it into my skin, pushing his fingers into my mouth so that I tasted it again. Doing it aroused him more quickly than normal and he began to move himself up until his groin was level with my head.

'His erection was half grown and his earlier aggression had gone. Without using words, his prick was asking politely to be sucked. More than that, it was begging to be sucked. I still didn't know how, but I leant forward and took it in my mouth, took all of it in my mouth so that it touched the back of my throat. The reaction was instantaneous. It grew and stiffened and swelled as if I had blown up a balloon and I removed my mouth to look at it. It was huge and I had done it. From the wood I heard another gasp.

'He attempted to put it back in my mouth but I turned my head. It was too big now and I didn't want him to shoot his sperm in my mouth, I still didn't like the taste. He didn't insist. Instead, he pulled up my dress again and rolled me onto my stomach. He lay on my back and used my buttocks, pushing his prick between my thighs so that it again looked as if he was inside me. He did this for a long time and I listened to his groans and to the softer groans that came from the trees.

'When he changed his position so that his prick was lying in the valley between my buttocks, I moved slightly so that I could stare surreptitiously into the trees. He had raised himself above me now, holding himself on his hands whilst his prick, which was very wet, slid between the globes of my bottom, and I knew it wouldn't be long before he came a second time.

'To me, what he was doing meant nothing, his growing urgency meant nothing. What excited me was the fact that I was watching one of the watchers. He had moved to get a better look and between the foliage of a bush, I could see him masturbating, timing his strokes to my boyfriend's strokes.

'At last my boyfriend came, the base of his prick pressed into the flesh of my buttocks so that his friends could watch him shoot his sperm up my back. As he came and I felt the hot drops on my flesh, the boy in the bushes came, his sperm flying out to land on the earth at his feet.'

Bianca gulped softly for saliva and licked her lips.

The Doctor said: 'Does the thought excite you still?'

'Yes.'

'Did it excite you then?'

'Yes.'

'Why?'

'Because I knew that later that night the boy would relive the scene in his bed, that they all would. I knew that when they were alone in the night they would all masturbate as they thought of me, that they would all imagine their pricks in my mouth and on my buttocks. I knew they all wanted me.'

'Were you tempted to let them have you?'

'Only in my fantasies.'

'Why not in reality?'

'Because I wouldn't have had control, because they

wouldn't have had control either. They were all virgins.'

'You said they all wanted you. Was it you that they wanted, or was it sex?'

'It was sex, of course. But I was the channel through which they dreamed they might attain it. It was the first hint at how powerful sex was, and what power it could give to those who knew how to use it.'

'But at this point in your life, it was the boyfriend who had the power?'

'Yes. He used it to show off to his friends. To give them a little treat.'

'Were you ever happy with him?'

'No, but at that age I don't think many young people are happy with their relationships. He was my boyfriend because it was necessary to have a boyfriend. I didn't like him but our relationship became a habit. Eventually I broke the relationship because it was becoming unsavoury.'

'In what way?'

'He used and abused me. I put up with that because I had begun to save those aspects of it that I could use for my own satisfaction. But I suspected he was planning to make me available to his friends as well. I think the only reason he didn't make me available to them was because if he had, they would have discovered he had never actually completed the sex act with me. That we were both virgins, too.'

'Do you still fantasise about the four boys all having you?'

Bianca smiled to herself.

'Sometimes.'

The Doctor said: 'Do you have any good sexual memories from this period?'

'Yes. There was another boy who was much more mature. He didn't live locally but was visiting friends. I only saw him once or twice. The second time we lay in the back of his car, on the seats.

'What did you do?'

'The usual things.'

'But this time you enjoyed them?'

'Very much. He made me horny and he didn't just take. He gave. He gave me the first orgasm I hadn't given myself.'

'Did you go all the way with him?'

'No. But he didn't mind. There were other things. Things he taught me.'

'What did he teach you?'

'How to use my mouth.'

'Did you use your mouth on him?'

'Yes.'

'Did he come in your mouth?'

'Yes.'

'Did you enjoy him coming in your mouth?'

'Yes.'

She remembered the heat inside the car, heat they had made themselves in the two hours they had touched, probed and licked each other's bodies. Her dress had been around her waist, the front open, her breasts exposed, her panties removed. And she remembered the smell.

He had come twice, once against her buttocks, and the second time in her mouth because he said he dare not put it near her vagina again for fear of making her pregnant.

Bianca had appreciated his concern and had used her mouth as instructed and had tasted his semen and, for the first time, appreciated it. The taste and texture and the way he had filled her throat hadn't been particularly pleasurable, but the way he had thrashed around and groaned had been a worthwhile experience and made her realise, again, the power she had over men.

'You said he gave you an orgasm? How did he do that?'

'I came three times. The first time against his mouth, the second time against his fingers and the third time against the edge of the seat as I sucked him.'

Bianca wished she was finished here and was back in the privacy of her hotel room so she could do something about the state she was in.

The Doctor seemed to sense her condition.

He said: 'I'll leave you alone for a few moments to recover, Bianca. When I return, we'll continue. But only if you feel up to it.'

She remained on the couch and listened to his footsteps as he left the room. The door shut behind him. Her fingers moved across her stomach and she came a fourth time in the back of the car.

Chapter 4

When the Doctor returned, Bianca had no objection to the continuation of her analysis. She was relaxed and looking forward to it, although his first question took her by surprise.

He said: 'When did you lose your virginity, Bianca?'

She hesitated.

'Bianca?'

'It was in the park.'

She returned in her mind to the shed that was filled with memories.

'With the boy in the rain?'

'No. After that. I was seventeen and I didn't want to be a virgin any more, but most of the boys I had been with didn't know how to do it. I wanted to learn how to do it properly.'

'What did you do?'

'I went back to the park, to see the gardener.'

The Doctor remained silent until Bianca continued to tell her story.

'It was the next summer, a year later, and it was raining again. I had been in the park since, and had seen the gardener, but at a distance. This time I went when I knew there would be nobody else around because of the rain. I wore a raincoat and carried an umbrella. I also prepared for the visit.'

She hesitated because what she was to say was blatant.

'Go on,' he encouraged softly.

'I knew the way men liked women to look. I had

seen pictures in magazines. So I bought a garter belt and stockings and wore high heels.'

She waited for admonishment.

The Doctor said: 'Did you buy these things specifically to visit the garden? Or did you buy them for the fantasy of visiting the garden?'

'I think, when I bought them, it was for the fantasy. I remembered the feeling of power in the back of the car, and I thought what it would be like to use that power over a man, a real man, with dirt on his hands and a brutish life. It was the fantasy.'

'Did you masturbate to that fantasy?'

Bianca licked her lips.

'Yes. I wore the clothes and masturbated to the fantasy in my room.'

'And how did the fantasy become real?'

'I went to the park three times before that happened. The first two occasions I watched him working from a distance, watched him go to the hut but didn't approach him, didn't let him see me. It excited me to watch him and know that all I had to do was make the approach. It was exciting to be this close, but each time I told myself there were too many people about. Instead I went home and masturbated.'

'But the third time?'

'The third time there was nobody about and I was so excited I was frightened. I told myself that this time I had to at least speak to him. So when he went into the hut, I went into the rose garden and I went into the hut as well. I pretended I hadn't known he was there and that all I wanted was to shelter from the rain.'

The gardener had been sitting on a bench in the darkness of the hut, an open bottle of red wine in his hand. Up close, he didn't look as old as she had imagined. Maybe twenty-five or twenty-six. He had been wearing gloves for his work and now he had taken them off and she had noticed his hands were clean.

'What happened?'

'He said it was alright for me to shelter. He offered me a drink of wine but I refused. I was standing by the door jamb where I had been with the boy, and he got up and stood in the doorway with me, leaning against the other door jamb. He said he remembered me, remembered that I'd been in the hut before with my boyfriend.'

She remembered the dialogue clearly.

Bianca said: 'He wasn't my boyfriend.'

The gardener said: 'He looked like your boyfriend. He was fucking you.'

'He wasn't.'

'It looked like it, from where I was.'

'He didn't know how.'

The gardener smiled, possibilities beginning to dawn.

'Do you know how?'

She was brittle with excitement at flirting this close to reality.

'No.'

'Do you want to know how?'

'Some day.'

He reached across and stroked her hair.

'Why not today?'

She couldn't speak. His arm was blocking the doorway and she couldn't run. She couldn't do anything but let him step close and put his arms around her and pull her tight against him and kiss her, hard and strong with an open mouth and a tongue that slithered over her lips and her face. The bristles on his chin rubbed her skin and his breath smelled of stale wine.

The Doctor prompted her: 'What did he do?'

'He unfastened the raincoat and put his arms inside it and felt my body. When he discovered I was wearing a garter belt he grinned. He knew I had put it on for him.'

'The gardener's hands traced the outline of the straps of the garter belt before cupping both of her buttocks. He held her against his groin and leaned away to leer into her face.

'You really do want fucking, don't you?'

She was rigid with fear and anticipation. Her eyes were wide and staring. He licked his lips.

'Get this off.'

He pulled her raincoat from her shoulders and she let him remove it. He threw it on the bench where he had been sitting and put his hands up her dress, running his palms along the back of her thighs from nylon to flesh to nylon panties. He kissed her again, wet and slobbering, his tongue licking her face as well as inside her mouth. He was excited and panting, one hand gripping a buttock, the other rubbing between her legs at the front of her panties.

She remained in shock.

He held her skirt up and leaned away to look at her legs in the white stockings. He swore and pushed a hand inside her panties, running one finger into the groove of her sex. She was dry with fear and gasped. He grinned.

The gardener moved Bianca to the bench and he made her lay down on it, throwing her skirt around her waist. He knelt and pulled down the panties.

As they began to slide past her hips, she held them momentarily, her last resistance. Then she let the nylon slip from her grasp and he took them off. He opened her legs and put his head there and the slobbering mouth and tongue made her wet and made her arch from the bench and the tongue dug inside her and she came.

The orgasm was fierce and shocked them both. As it subsided, she saw him standing by her side, unfastening his trousers and unleashing his weapon. He began to arrange her legs and she awoke from the fantasy and shook her head.

'Go on, Bianca.'

'He took off the raincoat and lay me on the bench and removed my panties. He used his mouth because I was dry and I came. Almost straight away, I came. Then he took out his prick and was preparing to have sex with me but I stopped him. I said he could only do it if he wore protection, a condom. I didn't want to get pregnant. He tried to persuade me to let him do it and said he would be careful but I refused. I think he thought that if he insisted I might scream rape, so he agreed not to do it this time, and that he would bring with him a packet of condoms the next time. Because he was so reasonable, it made me feel safe.'

The Doctor said: 'What did he do instead?'

'He put it in my mouth and I sucked him until he came.'

Bianca hadn't enjoyed the taste but she had enjoyed the power of having this big brute of a man at her mercy simply by using her mouth on his most sensitive part.

'Did you go back?'

'Yes. The next time it rained. That was the arrangement. I wore the same clothes and went at the same time and he was waiting. He showed me a packet that contained three condoms. I didn't speak, I just nodded.

'He took off my raincoat and hung it on a hook. This time he was prepared and had an old mattress which he had covered with a blanket. He closed the door of the hut and the only light came in from small windows high in the walls near the roof. He wanted to take my dress off and I said no but he insisted so I let him. He lay me on the mattress and stood over me, looking at my body. It was as if he couldn't get enough of just looking, drinking me in with his eyes, having sex with his eyes.'

She remembered the smells of the mattress, the blanket, the damp, the earth; she remembered feeling so excited that she could have fainted.

'The gardener took off all his clothes but his shoes and his socks, and lay down on the mattress with me. He kissed me and touched me. He wasn't gentle. He was in possession of me, he didn't have to be gentle. He removed my brassiere and sucked my breasts. He removed my panties and sucked me between my legs and pushed fingers inside me. I didn't come this time. This was preparation and I let him lubricate me. When he was satisfied, he rolled a condom onto his prick and got between my legs and pushed inside.

'I was expecting pain but there was no pain. There was discomfort and an unexpectedness about it. That he was so big and so hot. He held it inside me without moving and let me get used to its size and, I think, because he was so excited he was in danger of ejaculating. Eventually he began to thrust, to fuck me. He didn't take long, even though he tried to make it last. He kept me in the hut for an hour, until he had used all three condoms.'

The Doctor coughed.

'Did you enjoy the experience?'

'I don't think enjoyment is the correct word. It wasn't enjoyment; it was sex. Dirty and sometimes painful when he pushed me into positions that hurt. But it was sex that filled me.'

'Filled you?'

'Well, fulfilled me. It fulfilled me at that time after being with boys who only knew how to rub themselves to orgasm.'

'Did you come?'

'Not then. I was too aware of the experience, the situation. I wanted to learn.'

'You said not then. Did you see the gardener again?'

'Oh yes. Almost every time it rained that summer I went back. Fourteen times in all. The next time I went, he introduced me to his foreman. She smiled. 'He said we had to let the foreman watch so we could continue using the hut.'

'Did you let him watch?'

'Yes. He was an older man. About fifty. At the time, he seemed incredibly old. He was a short man, bald but not fat. Being a gardener had kept his body firm. He was very strong. He had a big black moustache. I was nervous when I met him and so, I think, was he. He didn't say much, he never said much, but he shook hands with me when we met. Then he sat on the bench while the gardener took off his clothes and undressed me and put me on the mattress.

'I was nervous again, but a different sort of nervous, another facet of excitement, I suppose. The gardener did things to me and I kept sneaking looks at the foreman. He was conscious of me looking at him and tried not to show reaction. But when my head was down while I was sucking the gardener, I heard the foreman grunt and move on the bench. Then, when the gardener was taking me from behind, the foreman gave up any pretence. He took his prick out of his trousers and masturbated.'

This time Bianca couldn't resist. She rubbed her thighs together at the memory of her power over men. She had been an unsophisticated seventeen-year-old with coltish legs and small high breasts, who had worn a woman's garter belt and white stockings to gain tuition in sex and had, in the process, made two conquests. Even the choice of white had been calculated to reflect her virginity.

The Doctor coughed again to clear his throat.

'Did he do anything else, other than masturbate?'

'Of course. The foreman said it was my fault I had

got him so excited. Therefore I should give him relief. I knelt in front of him and used my hand, as I had used it on boys, and watched his eyes glaze. Then the gardener knelt behind me and pushed inside again. I could feel him shaking with the new excitement of sharing me and I remembered the faces of the boys on the lawn, how dry-mouthed they had been, how desperately they had wanted me. The gardener pushed my head down and I took the foreman's prick in my mouth. It was short and very thick with a bulbous purple head. I only had to suck it a few moments before he came.

The Doctor got to his feet. His voice was low.

'Excellent, Bianca. Excellent. If you'll excuse me just a moment. Please remain on the couch. I think you need a few minutes to collect your thoughts before we continue.'

He left the room, closing the door behind him, and she was alone. Her hand slid between her legs and she touched herself to ease the itch.

The gardener had been rough but the silent foreman had been gentle. That afternoon she had stayed in the hut for two hours while they used her, together and separately. They rested in between orgasms, but she got no rest. It was the start of an idyllic summer.

Strangely enough, she didn't orgasm on that occasion either. The experience was too new and she wanted to remain aware. But on the occasions afterwards, she learnt to come quickly and to take her time, to fake it and to make it simultaneously with her partner.

She also learned that men had fantasies as strong as her own. They bought her underwear and stockings and she dressed for them so they could take it off. The gardener liked black and red but the foreman preferred white.

When she said she was still at school, they asked her to bring her school uniform and she did, wearing a shirt and tie, grey pleated skirt and maroon blazer with white ankle-socks.

That afternoon, the first time she wore her uniform, they were so filled with desire that they kept her in the hut until it went dark. That afternoon, she came seventeen times, once for every year of her life.

Her finger was digging urgently through the silk of her dress when the door opened and the Doctor returned.

'I think that's enough of memories for today, Bianca. You've been very good, very forthcoming. And you will get better.'

He went to sit behind his desk. She sat up shakily, swung her legs to the floor, and returned to the armchair where she had been sitting before.

'How do you feel?' the Doctor said.

'I don't know.' She laughed nervously. 'Odd.'

'Horny?'

He was smiling, his eyes wide and honest.

'Yes. Horny.'

'Good. Very good. But now we enter radical areas. Cosmo explained?'

'He said you were unorthodox.

'Well, that's one way of putting it. What I like to do is present my patients with a series of tests. The first one you passed exquisitely by the way you have dressed. You are extremely beautiful.'

She blushed.

'Thank you.'

'Would you stand?'

Bianca got to her feet hesitantly.

'And would you raise your skirt and show me your underwear?'

'I beg your pardon?'

'You heard what I said, Bianca. Please comply.'

This was unexpected and embarrassing, but Cosmo had said the Doctor was unorthodox. She raised her skirt slowly and he watched until it reached her waist, revealing pale blue silk French knickers and garter belt, and long tan hose that melted into the tan of her flesh.

He smiled gently.

'There's no need to blush, my dear. You're very beautiful. That's fine.'

He indicated with a finger and she dropped her skirt back into place, relieved and at the same time aroused at showing herself to a stranger.

'The next stage of your treatment takes place immediately. You have so far sampled the first taste of my methods and if you feel you are unable to comply with the treatment I recommend, you may, of course, abandon it at any time without recrimination. Do you wish to continue?'

He smiled and waited and she gulped.

'I want to continue.'

'Good girl. Then you will leave here with your brother-in-law. I have given him instructions which you must follow to the letter. Tomorrow, you will return here for another session on the couch.'

'Where are we going?'

'Into a new world of sensuality, my dear Bianca. And I think you will enjoy it.'

Chapter 5

Cosmo took her to a dress shop that was within walking distance of the doctor's house and they looked through racks of garments. She wondered why he had brought her there. He pointed to an attractive black dress and suggested she try it on.

The fitting rooms were at the rear of the shop. They climbed two carpeted steps and entered a long room. The far wall was mirrored but three cubicles lined each of the side walls, heavy draped curtains ensuring their privacy. He indicated the end cubicle on the left and she entered and took off her dress. As she hung it up, Cosmo opened the curtain wide. She started with shock and covered herself with her hands.

'No false modesty, Bianca. The Doctor says you must learn to display yourself.'

Cosmo was looking at her with passive eyes that were no intrusion, but she could see the reflection of a young man in the mirrored wall. He was near the entrance to the fitting rooms, sitting in a chair, waiting for someone. It was as if her stare alerted him and he turned his head and their eyes met in the glass. Bianca took a deep breath, licked her top lip and overcame the urge to cover herself. She put her palms on her hips and stared at the young man.

He looked away and then back and she held his gaze again for a second, before turning to give him a different view, and taking the black dress from the hanger and trying it on.

The dress was shorter than she normally wore but

Cosmo approved, so she removed it, still with the curtain open, still with the young man staring at her reflection, and put her own dress back on.

When she came out of the cubicle, the young man was with a girl who could have been his sister. They were being attended by an assistant at a till.

She and Cosmo joined them and waited while the girl paid for a skirt. All the time she watched the young man, her face expressionless. His gaze dropped fleetingly from her eyes to her body and back again to her eyes. She licked her lips; she was shaky with excitement at the interest she had aroused.

The girl started to leave the shop and had to nudge her brother to gain his attention to go with her. Cosmo paid for the black dress.

They also left the shop and she took deep breaths of the warm summer air. It was like being a child again and playing games. No, not a child, a young girl who was delving innocently into sex and discovering how superior it was to ponies.

She remained isolated by language and by physical presence. The sex was in her head and on her lips and in her body and in other people's eyes. She could feel it in her thighs and her tummy as she walked.

Cosmo left her at a metro station and said he would call her later at the hotel. He bought her a ticket and pointed out the route she should take on a wall map of the system so she wouldn't have to attempt to converse with anyone, and she went below ground on an escalator busy with people.

As she hesitated at the junction of two tunnels, she became aware that she was being followed. The young man from the shop had also stopped, ten yards away, and was pretending not to notice her.

Another part of the Doctor's plot?

She found the platform she needed and he stood close by in the crowd. In the shop she hadn't noticed what he looked like, simply that he was young. What she had noticed was the way he had gulped several times as he had appraised her body, and that the sight of it had aroused him because he had uncrossed his legs and had adjusted himself in his trousers.

Now she tried to fix his features in her mind. He was perhaps twenty-two or twenty-three, a little taller than her, and slightly built. He wore blue jeans and a black leather jacket, he was clean shaven and his hair was thick and black and swept back in heavy folds. He wasn't handsome and he wasn't ugly, she decided. What struck her most was that he was young and his eyes were curious.

When the train arrived, he followed her on board. There were no seats and she stood by a door, hemmed in by bodies, and held onto a hanging strap. By the time the train had reached the next station, the young man was behind her. She had followed his progress in the reflection of a glass partition.

There were four stations before she had to change. People looked into space, bored with their thoughts; some tried to read, others stared at the advertisements above their heads.

His hip was against her buttocks. The train was crowded and it was excusable. It pressed harder with the lurch of the train. Her lips were dry again and she licked them and didn't move away.

His touch was not unexpected but still made her hold her breath. For a second she couldn't identify what part of him was touching her, before she realised it must be the back of his hand. It was against her bottom. Because of the crush, it was still excusable.

The train stopped and there was an ebb and flow of passengers and she moved backwards slightly to make room for those who had boarded. The train started and she moved again to keep her balance and his hand turned.

His palm lay against a buttock.

This time there was no mistake, no justification. It was not excusable.

Bianca concentrated on continuing to breath normally. She was safe, she was under the orders of the Doctor. She should look forward to being praised for the way she was accepting the tests he had set. The young man's actions obviously had prior approval therefore it was outside her control. She had no decisions to make about his behaviour, she had simply to accept it.

There were three stations until she had to change.

The hand gained confidence by not being reprimanded. It moved slowly, defining the curve of her buttock, the tips of the fingers being the sensitive vanguard of a gentle exploration.

Bianca's mouth was dry. She gulped and licked her lips and looked at the bored humanity around her. No one could see what was happening. The young man was extremely discreet and they were hidden on one side by a partition between the standing area and the seats, and on the other side by the dress-shop bag that she held in her left hand.

The train rushed unexpectedly into the next station and she moved backwards slightly in surprise, her right buttock moving onto the hand that tensed against the softness, her left buttock against the hardness at his groin.

She automatically moved forward a fraction to reduce the contact and the train stopped and there was another ebb and flow of passengers. He didn't move, as if waiting for her to indicate she was still prepared to undergo the test.

Doors closed, sealing them in, the carriage lurched and she swayed with it, backwards against him.

Two stations until she had to change.

A businessman was standing at an oblique angle in front of her, unaware that the edge of his briefcase was pressing against her thighs.

She moved her buttocks backwards slightly against the young man, and then briefly forwards to put the confluence of her thighs against the briefcase.

Bianca's mouth opened at the electricity that passed through her body as the hard edge of the briefcase touched her vagina. The afternoon's confessions, her exhibitionism in the dress shop, and being touched in a crowded train had inflamed her senses.

The young man changed his position and now his erection lay in the valley between her buttocks, his fingers stroking, through the silk of the dress, a strap of the garter belt. He held his upper body away from her so that to casual observers they remained strangers – which, Bianca told herself, they were; total strangers sharing a journey that made her prickle with desire.

He moved imperceptibly against her buttocks, pushing her just as imperceptibly against the briefcase. She stifled a moan in her throat. He increased the pressure, moving the hardness in a long and deliciously slow grind that caused his fingers to splay against her thigh in pleasure. She gulped and her knuckles were white as she gripped the hanging strap.

This time a moan did escape but it was lost in the roar as the train entered another station.

They stayed as they were until the shifts of commuters had changed over, even though there was no longer any need for them to be this close. People were still standing but there was more room now and the briefcase moved away and she felt like she had lost a lover.

Bianca had to change trains at the next station. Did the young man know?

He renewed the long, slow grinds that he achieved

by the contraction of his stomach muscles and hips, and she attempted to assist by moving her buttocks.

By the time they roared into the next station she could feel his urgency building; his breath had become ragged. She half turned her head, not to look at him, but to give him an indication that she had to go, and smelled peppermint from his mouth.

He stopped and the train stopped and, as the people moved, she let herself go with them on legs that quivered.

Bianca let the flow take her along a platform but, when the crowd had dissipated into different echoing tunnels, she found another wall map of the metro system. She inspected it while she rested.

The young man was still with her. He waited two yards away, hands in the pockets of his leather jacket. Her glance acknowledged him but didn't remain on him; she didn't want it to be intimidatory. It confirmed her earlier impression of youth and eagerness without identifying whether he was handsome or indifferent.

She stared at the wall map, located where she was with a finger, and traced out the three stops to where she was going. She tapped her destination. Now he knew.

In her eagerness to start the final stage of her journey, she got lost in one of the endless tunnels, regained her bearings, and joined a throng heading the correct way.

Her train ride so far had been around the suburbs. Now she was heading into the city and had joined a surge of travellers.

Bianca pushed to the edge of the platform. The young man was directly behind her. She was becoming anxious in case she couldn't claim a suitable place when the train arrived. She chewed her bottom lip and watched the mouth of the tunnel and heard the warning rumble.

The train arrived, hissed to a halt and the doors slid open. She exchanged pushes with those who were disembarking, boarded and found herself adrift in the crowd. Being a beautiful woman gave her an advantage in moving between the bodies but she was unable to gain the position she wanted. The young man had also had difficulties and was trapped sideways to her.

The doors closed, the train moved, the bodies lurched and she stared ahead and smelled the peppermint from his breath as he gazed at her profile, and felt the fierceness of his erection pressing into her thigh.

Anger calmed her. Their fellow travellers were enemies, out to thwart an essential experiment. It would be necessary to take the initiative.

At the next station she anticipated the inevitable lurch and the press of those attempting to get off and, pretending to lose her balance, she pushed the young man sideways and followed him as the mass of people became fluid.

A woman frowned at her and two men winced at having their toes stepped on, but she smiled an apology. The men accepted it, the woman did not but Bianca didn't care. She had attained a similar position to which she and her stranger had occupied on the previous train.

They had two more stations together.

Bianca was elated at her achievement. They were legitimately crowded together and shielded from sight from the waist down by the partition and the dress bag.

The train started and the young man replaced his erection into its groove as if it had seigneural rights, and his hand held her hip possessively. His thrust was still discreet but more urgent and she attempted to aid him by pushing backwards.

She listened to his breathing and turned her head slightly, as if staring at one of the ceiling advertisements, to smell the peppermint. His movement was infinitesimal and his rhythm constant. His hand roved her thigh.

The next station came and they both waited impatiently for the train to start again so that the conclusion could begin.

Passengers changed and a pretty secretary wearing a business suit with a tight skirt was pushed face to face with Bianca. She held a document case across her breasts and she smiled at Bianca, a quirky smile that said: hello for the next few minutes that we'll be together and sorry if I'm crowding you.

Bianca twitched a smile back that said: don't speak, I won't understand, I don't want to understand.

The carriage was back in motion and so was the young man. His hand went beneath her skirt and was suddenly touching the flesh of her thigh and she gave an involuntary gasp and noticed the secretary was looking curiously straight into her startled eyes.

Bianca held the secretary's gaze, her own eyes curious about the girl and openly reflecting the lust she felt. She wondered about the secretary's sex life and whether she had had many lovers. Her eyes flickered to her hand and saw no wedding ring and flickered back to her face. Did that mouth do lewd things with men? Did those limbs open at their touch and did she moan in orgasm?

The young man's fingers dug into the soft flesh of her bottom before gripping her hip as he came in his trousers, his erection hard and pushing in the valley of her buttocks.

Bianca locked eyes with the secretary, as if the two of them were having sex, let a sigh escape from her open mouth, and touched her top lip with her tongue.

She let the tension ease from her face as the young man sagged behind her, and smiled at the secretary, her mouth still open, satisfaction in her eyes. The secretary blushed and licked her lips.

Their destination arrived, and she left the train without looking back, climbed stone stairs and emerged into fresh air and daylight. The hotel was a block away and she walked towards it quickly, wanting to lock herself in her room, to pick over the memories of the afternoon with her fingers.

Behind her, the young man trailed as she knew he would, but she sensed this was as far as the test would go today. On the steps of the hotel she turned and looked but he was already crossing the road, pausing on a traffic island to stare back.

Their eyes locked as they had in the dress shop an experience ago.

Next time, her eyes said.

He nodded, as if in reply.

Chapter 6

Bianca wore a beige dress in madras cotton for her visit to the Doctor the following day.

She wore no brassiere beneath the loose bodice. Her breasts were full and firm and she enjoyed the feeling of freedom. The skirt was knee length and she wore tan stockings and underwear, and low sandals in natural leather.

Cosmo approved when he collected her from the hotel and so did the Doctor when he welcomed her to his consulting rooms and invited her to lie, once more, on the couch. He, again, sat out of sight near her feet.

He said: 'Relax Bianca. We made great progress yesterday. You were very good, very forthcoming. Try and regain the same comfort with your thoughts.'

He allowed the silence to settle and she again felt her tensions slip away and looked forward to the memories he might provoke.

The Doctor continued in a low and gentle voice.

'Tell me about your childhood, Bianca. Your family. Where you grew up.'

'I had no family. No immediate family, that is. My parents divorced when I was young, my father went abroad and we never heard from him again. My mother died when I was eight and I went to live with an aunt and uncle. They were much older than my mother.

'My uncle had a big house in the country outside Florence. We owned land. He had been a lawyer but was retired. My aunt died when I was eleven and he didn't really know what to do with me. That's why I went to boarding school.'

The Doctor said: 'It must have been strange for a young girl growing into womanhood, sharing a house with an older man.'

'It wasn't strange to me. That was all I knew and I was grateful to him for looking after me. He was a good man.'

'Was he much older than you?'

'When I was seventeen, he was sixty-five. Our birthdays were in the same month and I remember sixty-five being a milestone.'

'Did your uncle ever approach you sexually?'

'No.'

'Was there any sexual tension between you?'

'Yes. When I got older. On holidays from school. I suppose it was a shock to him that I grew so quickly from a child into a young woman. He didn't see me for months and then I turned up with breasts. I was also getting interested in sex at that time.'

'Did it cause any problems?'

'Not for me. But, yes, for him.'

'How?'

'I didn't appreciate the way I looked when I was in my late teens. I felt uncomfortable with my body, I wanted larger breasts, fleshier legs. But looking back, and from photographs taken at the time, I now know I was very attractive. My presence must have been disturbing to him. I was a temptation.

'I was careless about undressing and closing doors, and about the sort of clothes I wore if there were just the two of us in the house at night. I became aware of the way he looked at me. No, not at me, the way he looked at my body. I enjoyed it. It was flattering and made me feel like a woman. I became more careless.'

'Did your carelessness culminate in something more?'

'Yes.'

'At whose provocation?'

'Mine.'

'Tell me, Bianca.'

She paused to place the sequence in the right order in her mind, and the Doctor waited.

Bianca said: 'It was the year I was seventeen and he was sixty-five. The year I lost my virginity to the gardener in the park. That summer had filled me with sex so much I thought of nothing else.

'I had no desire to return to the park when summer ended. That was a chapter that had closed. But I was eager for further experiences. The idea occurred when I went home from school for the Christmas holidays. What better present to give my uncle?

'He hadn't made any women friends since my aunt died and I had the impression that they hadn't had much of a sex life anyway. But he was a man and I knew from the way he looked at me that he could still be aroused. He was kind and gentle and safe, but his health was not good and I thought he deserved some comfort in his old age and I had nothing else to give.

'It happened one night when there was a storm. I used the thunder as an excuse to go into his bedroom and said I was frightened. I was wearing a short nightdress and nothing else. He sat in bed and comforted me for a moment and when the thunder came again, I pulled back the covers and slipped into bed with him. Neither of us spoke.'

The memory was vivid.

His pyjamas were blue-striped silk. His breath smelled of toothpaste. She pressed her body against him and he couldn't hide his erection. Bianca was surprised. It felt enormous against her leg. The thunder rolled again and she moved in response. Her nightdress was around her waist and she rubbed her groin across the hardness and felt it quiver. He stifled a groan and tried to push her shoulders away but she nestled her head against him and wouldn't move. His heart was racing beneath her breasts and she hoped she wouldn't cause him to have a seizure.

Uncle kept pushing her away, so she turned over with her back to him, but pulled his arms around her.

'Please,' she said.

Slowly, he rolled onto his side and cuddled her. As he got used to her presence, she moved her body so that her naked buttocks were against his hardness. He didn't pull away. With each development in the storm, she moved against him, pulled a hand over her breast, rubbed her bottom against his hardness.

The Doctor said: 'Did you seduce your uncle?'

'No. I got him to put his arms around me so that he had to touch me. My bottom was against his prick, my breast was in his hand. He came in his pyjamas and I fell asleep.'

'Did it happen again?'

'Yes. Every night for the next week until I went back to school. We didn't say anything, didn't speak about it when it was happening or afterwards. During the day, he never tried to touch me. It was a nighttime secret, a dream that happened in the dark that was never acknowledged.'

'Did it develop?'

'You mean did he do more than just come in his pyjamas?'

'Yes.'

'Yes, it developed.'

The next night she wore the same nightdress and slipped into his bed without pretence. He remained lying on his back but when she snuggled close and slid a leg across his thighs, she felt his erection as big and stiff as ever. They remained like that for several minutes and he took no initiative.

She slid her leg away and casually rested her hand over his prick, as if she didn't know what it was and she was simply getting comfortable in bed. Her fingers stroked it with the sort of absent meanderings with which someone might caress the corner of a pillow. It pulsed through the silk beneath her palm.

Feigning restlessness in sleep, her hand became entangled with the pyjama cord and unfastened it. The pyjamas had been breached and the erection released. Her fingers gently scratched his stomach and his prick rested against the back of her hand.

Bianca rolled on her side again, presenting the naked buttocks the gardener and the foreman had both enjoyed, and upon which several boyfriends had spilled their seed. She took her uncle's hand with her in her sleep, pulling him onto his side, to lie against her.

She feigned snores and moved her nakedness against his nakedness. For the first time, he moved of his own volition. Tentative quivering strokes. She yawned and stretched her legs and his prick slipped between her thighs and she pulled his hand against her breast. His thrusts were still tentative but gained momentum. They lasted several minutes, each one towards the end accompanied by a small sigh, until he came with a choking noise in his throat and she allowed him to slip away and resume his prone position. Bianca smoothed his sperm into her skin and went to sleep.

Each night Bianca pretended to be asleep while he found relief upon her body. Each time, her uncle became bolder, taking longer.

The third night, she lay flat on her stomach, her arms outspread like a sacrifice, and he lay upon her back and used her buttocks for a full thirty minutes before coming.

The fourth night he penetrated her, causing her to bite her pillow at his size, and he came quickly. Later, she awoke to find him lying on her stomach, her legs wide and his prick inside her again. His eyes were closed, his face strained, and she closed her eyes as well, to maintain the pretence that neither of them knew what was happening. It was a long time before he came.

The last night he rolled her about the bed and took enough enjoyment to last him through the winter. All the while her eyes remained closed and although her body was compliant, she moved as if she was drugged. In the morning, while it was still dark and he was asleep, she went beneath the covers and took him in her mouth and gave him a final present.

'How far did it develop?'

'He fucked me.'

'Did you actively participate?'

'No. I used my body to provoke him but I pretended to be asleep through everything he did. He knew I wasn't asleep, but he could pretend I was. That way, it didn't complicate our smiles at breakfast. There was never any inference or suggestion, in word or touch, to suggest that it had happened.'

'Did it happen again, the next time you were at home?'

'On occasions. If I felt in the mood to be used. If I was receptive to his loneliness.'

'Did he take precautions when he had sex with you?'

'He didn't wear anything.'

'Didn't it worry you that he might make you pregnant?'

'I thought that at his age he wouldn't be capable of making me pregnant, or that if he believed himself to be capable, he would take precautions. He never did. He and my aunt never had children; perhaps he wasn't capable of fatherhood.'

'Did you ever orgasm on these occasions?'

'Never. That wasn't the point.'

'What was the point?'

'Being able to arouse him every time I got into his

bed, simply by being there.'

'You derived pleasure from that?'

'Yes. The pleasure was the power. Later, in my own bedroom, I would look at my body in a mirror and touch it where he had touched it and become aroused. Then I would use my fingers and make love to myself.'

'Did you masturbate a great deal?'

'Yes.'

'Do you still masturbate?'

'Yes.'

She rubbed her thighs together slightly.

The Doctor coughed.

'Are you feeling aroused now?'

'Yes.'

'If you wish, Bianca, you may masturbate while we talk. Would you like to?'

'I don't think so.'

'As you wish.' He paused. 'When did you learn to masturbate?'

'At boarding school when I was sixteen. My best friend, Kezia, showed me how.'

'Tell me how it came about.'

'It was at the start of a new term. We shared a room and she couldn't wait to tell me she had lost her virginity. A married cousin had done it to her during the holidays, and he had taught her how to make love to herself because he enjoyed watching her. She taught me.'

'Did you do it to each other?'

'Sometimes we would lie in bed together, for comfort. And sometimes we would talk about film actors and singers, saying who we liked and what we would like to do with them. We would take turns at pretending to be the famous man and we would pretend to make love.'

'How did you do that?'

'If I was the man, I would be in charge of what happened. I would kiss Kezia, stroke her body, kiss and suck her breasts. I'd lay on top of her, push my leg between her thighs, and press it against her. I would touch her between her legs, put my fingers inside and make her wet, and stroke her where she was most sensitive.'

'Did she orgasm?'

'Always. Sometimes several times.'

'Did she do it to you?'

'Yes. The same sort of routine.'

'Did you come?'

'No. I found it pleasurable but for some reason I couldn't come and I found it embarrassing to do it with her watching. I would wait until she was asleep or if she had gone to the bathroom and then would do it to myself, very quickly because I was so hot.'

'Have you ever come with a woman?'

'Yes, but it was much later.'

'Are you attracted to women?'

'Of course.'

'Sexually?'

'When you explore the heights of sexuality, gender has no meaning, bodies are simply bodies, with orifices and appendages to give and receive pleasure.'

'Very true, Bianca. But they don't sound like your words. Where did you learn this philosophy?'

She hesitated.

'From my husband.'

'Was your sex life with your husband full?'

'Very full.'

'How old were you when you met your husband?'

'Eighteen.'

'How did you meet?'

'At my uncle's house. Michel came for the weekend. He and my uncle went shooting, discussed business and signed a contract. Michel was buying land. I was on holiday from school. I could tell he was attracted to me.'

'Were you attracted to him?'

'Of course. He was a grown man, handsome and successful.'

'What did you do?'

'I made myself available. I made sure I was in places where I knew he would be, to give him the opportunity to take advantage of me. After all, I was a woman unhampered by virginity, but so far I had only had a gardener, a foreman and an old man.'

'Did you attempt to seduce him?'

'No. That was a thought that never entered my head. He was sophisticated and experienced. It was his duty to seduce me.'

'Did you tempt him?'

She hesitated at the memory and smiled.

'Yes.'

'What did you do?'

'I climbed a tree.'

'Tell me about it.'

Chapter 7

Bianca smiled as she recalled their first adventure together, and the satisfaction all the ones that followed had provided. She moved her thighs together gently. Even now, the thought of him turned her on.

'Michel arrived at the house on Friday evening and left on Monday. Each morning during his stay, he took a walk before breakfast in the grounds. When nothing had happened all weekend, I got up early on Monday morning and went out before him.

'The path he took went through a wood. I climbed a tree in the wood and I called to him when he approached. I said I was stuck and couldn't get down. He helped me down.'

Bianca had dressed with care in a light summer dress with a short full skirt that floated in the slightest breeze. She was nimble and had climbed to a branch that was head-height to Michel.

'What was your intention?'

'That he would be aroused by looking up my skirt and would seduce me.'

'What happened?'

He had enjoyed looking. Bianca remembered the smile on his face as she stared down at him from the tree branch. He had made no pretence.

Michel said: 'Why climb a tree this early in the morning?'

'I was looking for a nest.'

'And now you can't get down.'

'I don't know where to put my feet. Can you guide me?'

Bianca turned, holding onto the trunk of the tree, and her skirt billowed behind her. She lowered one foot and he guided it to a safe place; she brought the other foot down slowly to give him the maximum time to gaze up her skirt. He took hold of it and guided that to a safe place. His hands stayed on her ankles.

The exertion of climbing and the possibility of what he might do, took her breath. She moved her foot again and, this time, after guiding it to a lower branch, his hand went up her leg, beneath the skirt, to support her weight. He repeated the process with the other foot and now both his hands were on her legs.

She moved again, slowly, this time finding her own footholds and, by moving her body downwards, she moved his hands upwards, from stocking to flesh until they held her hips and he lowered her to the ground.

Bianca turned and he released her and the skirt fell into place. They were standing close and her face was upturned, her lips parted, waiting to be kissed.

He was no longer smiling but looking at her as if in calculation and indecision. Eventually, he smiled again, kissed her lightly on the lips, and continued on his walk.

The Doctor repeated his question: 'What happened, Bianca?'

'Nothing. He enjoyed looking up my skirt and he helped me down, but he didn't seduce me.'

'Were you very disappointed?'

'Yes.'

'What did you do?'

'That night, after he'd gone, I climbed into uncle's bed.'

'Why?'

'To punish Michel for not taking me. I dedicated to Michel all the things that uncle did to me.'

'Was it just to punish Michel?'

'No. It was also to prove I was a woman, no matter what he thought.'

'When did Michel seduce you for the first time?'

'Six months later.'

'Had you been with anyone else during that six months?'

'No. Not even uncle. I went back to school and he became ill. I left school to be with him, to look after him, but he died.'

Bianca sighed. She had been fond of him.

'The lawyer told me straight away that I was the sole heir. There was money and property, as well as the house. All of a sudden I really was a woman. I felt mature. For the first time in my life I was in control of my own destiny. There was no one to answer to except myself.'

'When did you see Michel again?'

'At the funeral. It was a small affair. Michel telephoned and offered his help with the arrangements but the lawyer had already taken care of everything. But when I knew I would be seeing Michel again, I wanted to make an impression. I bought new clothes, new lingerie, and had my hair styled.

'It's funny, but I was looking forward to this day of supposed sadness. For me it wasn't sad. I had mourned my uncle during his illness and I had repaid him for all his kindnesses with my body. The funeral was for other people, an occasion for them to remember a passing. It was a custom that had to be undertaken.

'There were fourteen people at the cemetery but Michel wasn't among them. I was upset and a woman touched my arm in sympathy and I wondered how she knew about Michel before I realised she was expressing sorrow about my uncle. The ceremony was brief and I shook everybody's hand as they left, and suddenly I was holding Michel's hand. He had been delayed and was apologising. He told me to stop smiling and then he took me back to the house in his car.

'I was wearing black, of course. A black dress, black underwear. It was the first black underwear I had bought and I had been excited when I went to choose it because I was choosing it for one purpose. In the car ride back to the house, I hoped Michel would like it. It never occurred to me that he would not now seduce me.'

Bianca paused, remembering the feeling in the pit of her stomach, her insides churning at the prospect of Michel inside her and making them churn even more.

The Doctor said: 'And did he seduce you this time?'

'Oh yes.'

'What happened, Bianca?'

'There was no one at the house. I had told the staff I wanted to be alone because I had anticipated Michel being with me. We didn't speak and he drove fast. I went upstairs to uncle's bedroom and Michel followed. He didn't know it was uncle's bedroom or that he had died in this bed, the same bed in which I had given him my body.

'We still didn't speak. He kissed me, softly at first and then ardently. And then he lost control and he threw me onto the bed and tore at my clothes. He ripped the bodice of my dress to expose my breasts and he pushed up the skirt to my waist. His mouth covered my mouth, and then my breasts, and he licked my thighs above the stockings and ripped the lace panties open because he was too impatient to take them off, and his mouth covered my vagina. I screamed and I came.

'He knelt on the bed between my legs and opened his trousers and released himself but I couldn't see it because of his clothes and then I felt it as he thrust inside me and I screamed again and I kept on screaming with every thrust until he came.

'We lay together for a short time after his first orgasm, uncomfortable and hot. We had generated so much sweat I could smell myself. He didn't undress himself and he didn't undress me. He started again by putting his prick in my mouth and I sucked it until it was hard. Then we continued fucking.

'That second time went on for almost an hour and, by the end of it, he had ripped off my dress and torn my camisole to the waist. The lace panties were around one thigh and both my stockings were laddered. He did everything to me. He fucked my mouth and my vagina and he sodomised me and I loved it.

'Later, I told him we were in uncle's bed and that I had dedicated all we had done to uncle. He laughed and asked why and I told him what I had done with uncle and it sent him wild and he started again. We made love, had sex and we fucked for two days. A week later, we were married.'

The Doctor said: 'Was the marriage happy?'

'Happy is the wrong word. It was complete. We loved each other and lusted after each other. We enjoyed all manner of sex together, all the time we were married. Our lust never faltered.'

She heard the Doctor get to his feet and walk behind his desk.

'I think that's enough talking for today, Bianca. I'll leave you alone for a few moments to compose yourself, before we move on to the next stage.'

He left the room.

Bianca continued to remember what she and Michel had done on her uncle's bed and her hand slipped beneath the wrap-over skirt. She pulled the inner part of the material to one side, and slipped a finger into the groove of her sex. Her buttocks contracted at the sensation.

Michel wanted to know in detail everything her

uncle had done to her and while she talked, prompted by his questions, Michel did things to her.

Later, they removed their clothes and she wore the short and flimsy nightdress she had worn for her uncle and Michel wore her uncle's silk, blue-striped pyjamas. They got between the covers and re-enacted every scene that he dredged from her memory from that first week when she had silently given herself to her guardian.

In between the narrative, she was required to feign sleep while Michel used the valley between her buttocks to masturbate or sucked her breasts or manoeuvred her legs with hands that were careful not to break the spell.

'Did he make a noise when he was fucking you?'

'Oh yes, he made a noise. He groaned as it went in and sighed as it came out.'

'Like this?'

Michel made noises.

'A louder groan and a longer stroke. A softer sigh.'

He tried again.

'That's it. Like that.'

The pyjamas still had the smell of her uncle and she was lost between dreams, the only reality being the pleasure between her legs and the way the man above her shook with urgency.

Beneath the skirt, her finger pressed and she came. Her body contracted around the pleasure zone and a groan escaped her throat. She wanted to do it again but the door opened and the Doctor entered the room and she moved her hand.

'You may get up now, Bianca.'

Bianca swung her legs from the couch, wondering if the flush she felt showed in her face. She put the finger she had used to her mouth and licked the tip.

The Doctor was behind the desk and he indicated an armchair and she sat before him.

'You were very good yesterday. I am pleased with the reports. I take it you were not offended?'

'No. I was not offended.'

'Good. Then we will move on. Cosmo will now escort you to another part of the house and introduce you to a colleague.'

'Is he a doctor, too?'

'No. But he helps me on occasions.'

'A specialist of some kind?'

'Yes. A specialist of some kind. He is the Blind Man.'

Chapter 8

The Blind Man sat in a darkened room. He was short and fat and sat in the middle of a chaise longue. His feet were flat on the floor, his legs splayed and he rested both hands on a walking stick and rested his chin on his hands.

Cosmo pressed a switch by the door that turned on a tall lamp that stood to one side of the chaise longue. It provided a spotlight of illumination. He left her and closed the door. Bianca waited, unsure what was expected of her.

The Blind Man raised a hand and motioned her to him. She walked across a wooden floor towards the pool of light.

She stopped in front of him.

He had a grey moustache and wore dark glasses. His hair was grey and thick and brushed straight back. He wore a black short-sleeved shirt that was buttoned to the neck and black trousers and shoes. His stick was white.

The Blind Man sniffed the air between them, his nostrils twitching and she thought he smiled. Could he smell that she had made love to herself?

He rested the stick in his lap and reached out to find her, holding her by the waist and moving her until she stood directly in front of him. She had to stand with her legs apart to avoid the walking stick. Her vagina was on a level with his face.

Her mouth was dry and she made moisture in it and licked her lips. There was a full-length mirror on the wall to her left and she stared at the bizarre tableau they made and waited.

The Blind Man put his hands behind her knees beneath the hem of the dress. His nostrils twitched again and Bianca imagined she could smell herself. The hands slid upwards, along the back of her legs, and she drew in a breath and stared into the mirror, surprised that she looked so startled, her eyes wide, her mouth in an O of anticipation.

When the hands reached the lace at the top of the stockings, they rested. His fingers were splayed, his thumbs upright, pointing the way ahead, his touch light. They moved again, but only slightly, so that they were half on the lace, half on the nakedness of her thighs, each thumb aligned against a strap of her garter belt.

The Blind Man flexed his hands to maximise the sensation. It was a gentle flexing and he repeated it several times. His thumbs stroked the silk straps of the garter belt where they held the stockings taut. She closed her mouth but continued watching their reflection in the mirror.

The hands moved, slowly but with purpose, and his palms and fingers seemed to expand with the curve of her flesh. There was no hesitation now, even as they slipped beneath the loose legs of her panties and caressed her buttocks.

They held the softness without demand, gaining their pleasure from the flexing of palms and fingers rather than the gripping of her flesh. Her vagina itched with want and she contracted her bottom without thinking and his hands read the movement.

They moved around the moons of flesh, following their contours, first from hip to valley, then from her waist to where the curves met the tops of her legs. He continued with the movements for several moments, until his hands were totally familiar with her contours.

His left hand became stationary, holding her right buttock. His right hand held the front of her right thigh. He stroked her leg for a while, from the lace top of the stocking to the silk of the panties, before continuing his upward caress. His fingers were gentle moles that delved into her pubic undergrowth, before becoming gentle talons that arched and scratched her lower abdomen.

Again, her buttocks contracted on the command of her vagina and she stopped looking into the mirror, hung her head and closed her eyes.

His little finger was the first to find its way into the top of the groove that led to her sex. It explored the first half inch with tantalising slowness. She tried to encourage it by moving her hips but it retreated.

Bianca opened her eyes with frustration but another finger took the initiative, slid over the top and across her clitoris to bury itself inside her.

She moved against it and it was joined by a second and a third finger. They had no difficultly entering because she was so wet. The Blind Man used the three fingers as one to drive in and out, whilst his thumb rubbed softly on the bud of her clitoris.

As Bianca moved against his hand, she became aware of the man's walking stick that still lay in his lap. The white stick had a black grip. It was thick and contoured to accept fingers, like the handle of a golf umbrella. The head of the grip was round and at its base there was a thick ridge to guard against a hand slipping.

She knew what was to happen next and the thought appalled and excited her. She wanted it to happen.

The Blind Man removed his right hand and the fingers of his left slid between her legs to maintain the attention at her vagina. He held the three fingers he had used in front of his face and his nostrils twitched. He wiped the fingers carefully on his moustache.

Now he picked up the white walking stick and Bianca

raised herself as he placed the round head of the black grip at the mouth of her sex. He paused but she couldn't wait and pushed herself upon it, feeling the contours ripple inside her. She swallowed the whole handle until its hard ridge was against her clitoris.

The Blind Man held the stick and she made love to it and, as she built to a climax, the fingers of his left hand, wet from their ministrations, slid along the valley of her buttocks and one inserted itself into her anus.

Bianca cried out and held onto his shoulders as she came, convulsing at the intensity. Strange noises escaped from her throat, inarticulate yelps and grunts that subsided as her shudders subsided. At last, her senses returned. Her mouth was open, her breathing laboured. She sighed.

He removed his hands and the walking stick. The suction of her membranes slurped as it came out. He hadn't said a word and he hadn't changed position and she knew it was over.

When she stepped back, she saw that he was holding the walking stick around its length. The black grip was before his face. It was smeared with white secretions.

Bianca looked at her reflection in the mirror. She saw a fully clothed and apparently respectable woman with a deranged expression. She took a deep breath, clenched her fists to reassert her identity, and walked back to the door to the accompaniment of her footsteps on the wooden floor.

Cosmo had gone and she was grateful she didn't have to face him. He had left her a ticket for the metro and she knew her way to the station. She welcomed walking back into isolation.

The young man was waiting near the station.

She saw him from across the street and her senses speeded up once more.

They ignored each other and she walked past him to stand at a wall map of the system. He didn't look over her shoulder to confirm her route. Instead, he moved a few steps away and looked along a side street, before glancing back at her.

Bianca looked in the direction he indicated. He began to walk and she followed, her breasts heaving beneath the thin material of the dress.

The street was narrow, the buildings tall. It was a residential street of apartments and the occasional shop or bar. They walked for perhaps a hundred yards before the young man turned off to the right, along a narrower street where there were tradesmen's yards and buildings that were closed and derelict.

He stopped abruptly and she inadvertently closed the gap between them before she, too, stopped. There were no other people in sight although she could hear the noise of a road drill and of traffic in the distance.

The young man glanced at her briefly, moved to a boarded building, pulled open a door and went inside.

For a second she was alone in tho street and wondered whether she should follow. It was a setting for a murder rather than a sexual experience. What if the young man became unstable and over-excited and failed to follow his instructions?

Bianca followed.

There was a staircase directly in front of her and she began to climb. It was an old building and the stairs creaked. The plaster of the walls had flaked. It smelled of failed lives and sadness.

There was no sign of the young man.

At the top of the stairs was a corridor that led to more stairs. Rooms led off the corridor. She looked into the first room and saw it had no outer wall. A demolition site lay beyond, and from it came the noises of workmen and a diesel engine that rattled. She hesitated at the next room.

It was empty apart from a kitchen table. Bare wooden floors and peeling wallpaper. There was a hole where the window had been and sunlight spilled through as if it were the mouth of God. The demolition sounds were more muted.

Hands gripped her shoulders and propelled her forward and she let out a yell and dropped her handbag. She was pushed against the table, and held herself upright by gripping it with her hands. A man pressed against her from behind and the fear and arousal was causing the muscles around her vagina to contract.

The skirt of her dress was pulled up and hands were on her flesh; impatient, seeking, demanding. They pulled aside her panties and found her wetness. The man gasped and she smelled peppermint from his breath. She heard the zip of his trousers open and then his hot erection was bludgeoning its way between her legs.

Bianca lifted herself and positioned her bottom to make the channel as receptive as possible and he held her open with rough fingers and pushed his prick inside.

He gasped loudly and her wetness squelched. He held her by the hips and heaved inside her – four, five, six times – and came, yelling over her back at the hole where the window had been as if God was sucking out his soul. He had come too quickly for Bianca and, as he yelled and pulsed, she pushed fingers onto her vagina and brought her own relief.

The young man withdrew and her skirt dropped back into respectability and she continued to breath deeply as she held herself over the table. She could hear him fumbling with clothes and a zipper but, as she turned towards him, he left abruptly without looking at her, without a word.

Bianca remained in the room until her breathing was back to normal. She brushed the dust from her dress and picked up her handbag. Her hands were still shaking and her legs felt weak. From the handbag she took a mirror and checked her make-up. Her lipstick was smudged where she had chewed her lip and she applied more.

The diesel engine that had been a constant background noise had stopped and she was suddenly aware of the silence. It frightened her. She could hear male voices, shouting to each other. They appeared to be coming closer.

She ran from the room and down the stairs, pushed open the door and stepped into the sunlit street. The young man was on the corner. He was waiting, hands in the pocket of his jacket.

Bianca knew, without being told, that the experiment was over and that he was now an anonymous escort back to the real world.

Chapter 9

Michel had taught her about the eroticism of clothes and she again took care before going to meet the Doctor the following day.

Bianca particularly liked silk for the way it felt and floated and she wore a two-piece red suit in the material with a blouson top that buttoned down the front and a skirt that lifted in the breeze.

Her underwear was also red silk, with the wide-legged panties her husband had said were so much more accessible for sex than briefs. They also made her feel permanently horny and gave her an edge over every man she met.

If they only knew . . .

She was still content to let her destiny be directed by the Doctor and continue to make no decisions. In a way, this bout of arranged sexual behaviour was like being back with her husband and when she returned to her hotel room after each engagement she watched one of the videos she had brought with her, one of the videos they had made together, and shared the experience with Michel.

The Doctor complimented her on the way she looked and they took their respective places, she on the couch and he in the chair near her feet. The couch was now familiar and represented the unwinding of memories that became more vivid in the telling as well as the slipway where fantasies were launched into reality.

They exchanged the pleasantries designed to put

her at ease before the Doctor's questions became more pertinent.

He said: 'Yesterday, you used a phrase to explain a sexual philosophy. You said when you explore the heights of sexuality, gender has no meaning. Bodies are simply bodies, with orifices and appendages to give and receive pleasure. You said your husband taught you this philosophy.'

'Yes, he did.'

'Is this a philosophy in which you still believe?'

'Yes.'

'Did it shock you, when he first explained it?'

'No, I think I had already discovered it, the summer I spent in the gardener's hut. Michel identified it, packaged it in words. He legitimised it. Having it identified and explained removed guilt.'

'Had there been guilt?'

'I had felt guilty at deceiving my uncle by telling lies about the days I spent in the gardener's hut. I felt guilty because I knew what I had been doing was outside the usual rules of propriety. But I never felt guilty about what I actually did. I enjoyed it too much to feel guilty.'

'If your husband had this philosophy of sexual liberation, why did he not seduce you that first weekend you met? The weekend you climbed the tree?'

'Because Michel was also a moral man. He was a guest in my uncle's house and my uncle was my guardian. To have taken advantage of me in those circumstances would not have been acceptable. It would have broken a trust.'

'But he took advantage of you after the funeral?'

'We took advantage of each other. I was my own guardian and we both knew what we wanted.'

'Does your philosophy have limits?'

'Of course. Michel enjoyed watching me have sex with other men and women, but I made love with only him. I could give my body to anybody but my soul was his property and his soul was mine.'

'You must have been very sure of each other.'

'We were.'

'You were married soon after the funeral.'

'Yes.'

'How long was it after you were married before your husband involved other people in your sex life?'

'A year.'

'Why did he wait a year?'

'He said the first year was ours alone. He also taught me how to dress, how to arouse men, how to masturbate and fellate them to provide maximum pleasure.'

'Did you enjoy that first year?'

'Very much. It was a graduation.'

'Did it upset you that after a year he wanted others to enjoy your body?'

'No. It was part of an ongoing process of discovery about ourselves and each other. I was nineteen and happy to have found a man I loved. But I realised there was a lot more of life to sample and I didn't want to miss any experience. It was exciting.'

'Did he prepare you for what to expect after the first year of marriage?'

'Oh yes. He said right from the start that he wanted to watch other men have me. When I told him about the gardener and the foreman, he was wild with desire and said he wished he had been there to watch.'

'You told him about the gardener and the foreman?'

'I told him about every sexual experience I had ever had. He wanted to know every detail, what I wore on each occasion, what the boys were like, where they came upon my body. He particularly liked hearing about the gardener and the foreman. He even took me back to the park so I could point them out to him. The gardener wasn't there but the foreman was. Michel had a video camera and filmed him.'

'Did he often use a video camera?'

'Yes. He made many films of us having sex. I still have them.'

'Do you still watch them?'

'Yes.'

'Do they arouse you?'

'Yes.'

'Do you masturbate while you watch them?'

'Yes.'

'When was the first time after your marriage that you had sex with someone other than your husband?'

'On our first anniversary.'

'Tell me what happened.'

'I had sold my uncle's house and property but we went back to the same area and stayed in a hotel. It was early September. On the morning of the anniversary, Michel wouldn't let me apply any make-up and he told me what clothes to wear. A thin white cotton dress that he had bought without my knowledge, white ankle-socks and flat shoes. He allowed me no underwear. He drove to the park where I had met the gardener.

'The day was warm and fine and there were other people walking in the park. They stared at me because it was possible to see through the material of the dress. They must have known I wore nothing beneath it. We walked to the rose garden. The entrance was through a gate in a brick wall. A notice on the gate said the rose garden was closed. Michel opened the gate, we went through, and he closed it again.

'Sprinklers were operating in the rose garden. Many of them. They were cascading water across the path that led to the hut. Michel told me to walk through the water to the hut. It was like walking through a tropical storm. My hair was plastered to my head, my dress became transparent and stuck to my body and my legs. He followed and got just as wet.

The door of the hut was partly open and he told me to enter. Waiting inside were the foreman and the gardener. Michel had found them and paid them. He had arranged everything.

'The same mattress lay on the floor, although it was covered by a clean sheet. A portable stove was in a corner and the hut was hot and humid. The foreman sat on the bench as he had the first time I'd met him. He even seemed to be wearing the same clothes. He looked embarrassed. The gardener was wearing jeans and a T-shirt. He had new tattoos on both his forearms. He grinned and licked his lips.' She smiled to herself. 'He actually licked his lips.'

She paused as she remembered the scene and the feeling in the pit of her stomach.

The Doctor said: 'Go on, Bianca.'

'Michel picked up a video camera that was already there, and began filming. The gardener and the foreman couldn't take their eyes from my body. I had filled out in the intervening two years. Then they had me.'

'How did they have you, Bianca?'

'The gardener started. He took off his clothes and he ripped my dress open. After he had me, the foreman had me. Then they had me together.'

A flush filled her cheeks as she remembered.

The gardener's erection was huge and for a few moments before he started, he masturbated as he looked at her body. The dress clung to every curve. It was taut across her breasts and her nipples were large and aroused and pushed impatiently at the material.

The hut was hotter now, with four of them cramped in it. Steam rose from both Bianca and Michel.

Then the gardener reached out and ripped the dress down the front with both hands. He ripped it to the waist and the violence of the act made Bianca gasp. He grabbed her breasts, mauling them, and he forced her to her knees and pushed his erection into her mouth.

She tried to put into practice what she had learned about fellating since she had last been with them, but he wasn't interested in finesse. He was crazy for sex, for her body. He acted as if he wanted it all at once, not knowing what to touch or grab next.

After only a few seconds in her mouth, he pushed her back onto the mattress and ripped the skirt of the dress, peeling the wet material from her legs. He crouched over her, pushed himself back into her mouth, and went down with his own mouth between her legs. He was hurting her, making her gag, but she was burning with sexual excitement and arched her hips to meet his mouth.

The water was turning into sweat and the sweat was mingling with the juices that were flowing from her vagina.

He moved again, knelt between her legs and thrust inside her. Even though she was lubricated it hurt and she cried out and he laughed, half-giggling, as if in hysteria.

Bianca began groaning, huge gulps of groans, and concentrated on coming before he orgasmed. She came and kept on coming as he pumped into her. Three of her orgasms ran one into the next until he came. Later, when Michel played the video, she was amazed at the noise they had made.

Lying on the couch, Bianca had the familiar itch between her legs that made her rub her thighs together.

The gardener rolled off and she was turned onto her stomach by the foreman. He knelt behind her, raised her hips, and entered her from behind. He lasted much longer, taking his time, breathing heavily, groping her body as he fucked her, his hands weighing her breasts in his palms as they dangled beneath her, squeezing and manipulating them. He was still using her by the time the gardener had recovered. The gardener knelt by her face and she sucked him back to solidity.

The Doctor said: 'What did they do to you?'

'Everything they had done before. From the front, from behind, in my mouth. Separately and both together.'

'And while they were doing this, what was Michel doing?'

'He was filming. He filmed everything.'

'How long did it last?'

'About an hour. The gardener came three times, the foreman twice. The gardener lay in the dirt on the floor still naked, the foreman sat on the bench, also naked. Then Michel had me. He put the video camera on a tripod and left it running, took off his clothes and lay down with me on the mattress.

'He sucked the men's sperm from my vagina into his mouth and kissed me with it. We shared it. Then he made love to me, quickly, and I came again.

'Later, in our room at the hotel, we watched the video and made love again and had sex again.'

Bianca heard the Doctor shift his posture in the chair.

'How often did you engage in sex with other people after this first occasion?'

'When the circumstances were right. When we felt like it.'

'How often?'

'Perhaps once a month. Perhaps three, four or even five times in a month. There was no timetable. Many of the occasions were arranged on the spur of the moment. Almost innocent.'

'Give me an example of almost innocent.'

Bianca smiled and remembered the hotel by the lake at Lausanne.

Chapter 10

Bianca said: 'It was one of the first occasions after our anniversary. We were staying in a hotel and a young porter couldn't keep his eyes from me. He was perhaps seventeen or eighteen, not much younger than me in age, but generations apart in experience. He was blond and good-looking and his looks were softened by his youth. He was a boy.

'Michel noticed the young man's interest and suggested it should be rewarded. I agreed. That afternoon, I remained in the room and Michel went out. He paid the young porter and gave him specific instructions. He told him that I had taken sleeping pills and was resting but that I had to be awakened at a certain time. Michel said he couldn't return to the hotel to wake me because he had an important meeting.

'He asked the porter to wake me. He told the porter to enter the room and shake me by the shoulder. After taking sleeping pills, he said, it was difficult to waken me and he should persist in shaking my shoulder until I was fully aware of my surroundings.

'When the time came for the boy to enter the room, I was lying face down on the bed. The bedclothes were on the floor as if I had kicked them there in my sleep. I wore only a short black silk nightdress.

'The boy first rang the bell but when there was no answer he let himself in. The door closed behind him. I heard him walk down the corridor and stop when he saw me. He gasped. After a few seconds, he moved again and walked slowly round the bed, as if on tiptoes. He was inspecting me from every angle. Then he spoke and said, "Madam", softly, not really wanting to disturb me. When I didn't respond, he said it louder and touched my shoulder.

'His first touch was brief and he pulled his hand away, as if he had been burned or received an electric shock. He said, "Madam" again, in a louder voice, and touched my shoulder again, shaking it gently. I still didn't respond. His hand remained on the skin of my shoulder. His fingers stroked my shoulder and my arm.

'The boy's breathing was shallow and ragged. He leaned towards me and I could feel his breath on my cheek. He kissed my shoulder with the touch of a butterfly. A little, damp, sensitive butterfly. It made me want to push myself against the bed to ease the itch. Instead, I moaned in sleep and opened my legs.

'I sensed that he had moved to the bottom of the bed. Then the hem of the nightdress was raised from my thighs. He was holding it up while he stared at my body. It was very difficult not to move beneath his gaze. He lay the nightdress at my waist, leaving me naked. For a while he simply looked, then his fingers touched and it was impossible not to move.

'I squirmed as if in sleep, opening my legs even further, and he pulled his hand away but this time it was only seconds before he replaced it and he felt my flesh, stroking my buttocks and my thighs. One finger stroked between my legs and I almost swooned. My vagina opened at his touch and I wondered if he had noticed.

'He removed his hands again and I heard him unzip his trousers. My mouth was dry. I hadn't expected him to attempt to enter me but I was glad he was going to try. But he didn't. I kept my eyes closed and listened to the sound of him masturbating. His breathing was ragged and the movement of his hand was making slurping sounds.

'The tension inside me was almost unbearable but I had to remain immobile, an object of his desire. It was difficult, and I squirmed again in pretended sleep, re-arranging my legs and rubbing myself against the mattress at the same time, and turning my head into the pillow to muffle the sounds I wanted to make.

'The movement caused the boy to stop masturbating. He said, "Madam" again, in an anxious voice that begged me to remain unconscious. I obliged. Then he knelt on the bed between my legs and I longed to move back and suck him into me, but I remained immobile although I couldn't stop the quivering of my buttocks.

'He supported himself with his arms on either side of me and lowered himself so that his erection touched me between the legs. I bit into the pillow and tried to stop myself from moving against him. He hung there, suspended on arms and knees, almost without breathing, and I had to move. I groaned in deep sleep, squirmed my buttocks upwards against his prick, and moved myself against it as if in a dream.'

Bianca was smiling at the memory, moving her thighs gently against each other.

The Doctor said: 'What happened, Bianca?'

'He came. The contact was all he needed. He tried to pull away but he couldn't stop his orgasm. I felt some of it splash onto my buttocks. Then he climbed off the bed and I heard his zipper and decided to wake up. I yawned and stretched and began to lift myself on my arms and he ran.'

He ran and she reached behind her to wipe the sperm from her buttocks with her fingers. She turned round on the bed and found the rest of what he had spilled. It lay in a trail across the sheet. There had been a lot. She lay down and licked at the pools of sperm, rubbing her face into its wetness, and she pushed the fingers that were sticky with his lust inside her vagina and came.

The Doctor said: 'And that was innocent?'

'It gave the boy pleasure and relief. He didn't even lose his virginity.'

'Did you enjoy the encounter?'

'Very much. So did Michel when I told him about it.'

The Doctor paused. Eventually he said: 'You have been even more forthcoming today, Bianca. You are sharing more of your memories instead of telling me some and saving the rest. Do you enjoy talking about them?'

'Yes.'

'Good. Do you want to talk some more?'

'Yes.'

'Very well. Tell me about the first time you had an orgasm with a woman.'

The villa was white, the sky an immense blue that drank the ocean from the lip of the horizon. The sun burned.

'We were on holiday. Michel had rented a villa that overlooked the sea. It was a large villa and we were there for a month. Friends stayed with us for the first week or so and, when they left, Michel became friends with two brothers we met in a bar in the nearby town.

'They were Norwegian and very blond, one nineteen and the other twenty-one, although they were so alike they could have been twins. Michel spoke to them in English. I can speak neither Norwegian nor English and never understood what they said.

'Every day, they came to the villa to swim in the pool and because Michel enjoyed the way they looked at me. At the villa, I sunbathed naked. They kept their shorts on, but I could see the bulges I caused.

'Michel suggested they find girlfriends and they did so. They brought two English girls and soon they were sunbathing naked as well. It was a stimulating few days, and Michel and I didn't mind if the couples went off to a bedroom in the afternoon or evening to have sex.

'The last day before the English girls went home was very hot. I went into the villa to have a break from the sun and Michel followed me. He, too, was naked. We stopped in a corridor and kissed and his erection grew instantly. We were both sweating and our bodies slid against each other.

'As we kissed, one of the girls came out of a bedroom. She had been putting oil on her body and her skin glistened. She apologised at interrupting but Michel smiled.

'He held me in his right arm and put his left arm around the girl's shoulders and brought her in to join us. It started as a friendly gesture, and he exchanged kisses with me and with her alternately. Kisses that were light and didn't mean anything. But the kisses began to change, and I put my arm around the girl and she reciprocated.

'In the course of the previous few days, the girl had enjoyed having sex with both the brothers and was sexually attuned. She was enjoying being kissed by Michel and so it was natural, when he moved our mouths together, that we should all kiss each other. Our tongues and mouths had no sex but were alive with sensitivity.

'While we kissed this way, his hands were stroking both our bodies and our hands did the same. He enjoyed having both our hands on his erection, but he moved so that the girl and I were face to face and he stage-managed our first kiss together. Our arms were wrapped around each other, our hot bodies slithered against each other, groin grinding against groin, and our tongues fought gently in our mouths.

The Doctor said: 'Did you enjoy it, Bianca?'

'It was wonderful. And while the girl and I kissed, Michel moved around us, kissing and licking our necks, moving his erection against my buttocks, against our thighs, then against her buttocks. Both the girl and I were groaning at the unexpectedness and pleasure of the encounter.

'What happened?'

'We moved into a bedroom. The shutters were closed against the sun and it was dark and cool, and the girl and I continued kissing and touching each other's breasts and buttocks, with Michel moving around us on the bed, touching and moving against us but not wanting to interrupt.

'I sensed the girl had never done this before and we reached a point where I had to take the initiative. I moved my mouth down over her breast and sucked her nipple and slid my fingers between her legs. She tensed for a moment and then relaxed, and I made her moan with my fingers before I went down all the way.

'At first she didn't want me to use my mouth and held me off but eventually she succumbed. I kissed her vagina as if it were a mouth and used her clitoris as if it were a tongue. She moaned and began moving. She couldn't control herself and she came.

'Her orgasm broke the barriers and I felt there was nothing we couldn't do together. I felt liberated at what I had done and I wanted her to do the same to me. She was persuaded to go down on me and, although she was hesitant at first, she soon became enthusiastic when she felt my reaction. I came quickly and pulled her up to my mouth so we could share the taste.'

The Doctor said: 'What was Michel doing all this time?'

'He was watching, moving around us on the bed, occasionally masturbating.'

'What happened then?'

'The girl and I did other things to each other. We put our breasts in each other's vaginas, we lay face to face and rubbed our groins together, we fitted our vaginas together by straddling each other with open legs. We mouthed each other at the same time. I remember burying my face between her legs as she licked me, overcome with the smell and taste and feel of sex, her wetness and juices all over my face and my hands pulling at her buttocks. It was glorious.'

'And you came again?'

'I came many times. So did the girl.'

'And Michel?'

'He came, too. After the girl and I had done everything together, he fucked us both and we shared his sperm when he came in our faces.'

The Doctor moved in his chair and allowed a silence to punctuate their conversation.

He said: 'Your memories are becoming more fluent, Bianca.' He stood up and his face came into vision near the foot of the couch. 'Your progress is accelerating but we will let the past remain the past for today. I'll give you a moment to yourself before I hand you back to Cosmo. He will provide an experience of the present.'

The Doctor left the room and Bianca sat up. She was aroused but she didn't touch herself. She knew she would receive satisfaction in what lay ahead.

Chapter 11

They went to a cinema that specialised in sex films. Cosmo bought tickets and led her through the foyer to where there was a choice of three small theatres. He held out a carrier bag.

'Put your handbag in here,' he said. 'You won't need it inside.'

They entered an auditorium and waited at the back until their eyes became accustomed to the darkness. A film was in progress and a naked woman was on the screen. The audience was small at this time of the day, a scattering of perhaps six men, all sitting isolated from any neighbour.

Cosmo led her a few rows down and as she passed one man she could see his hand moving beneath a coat that lay across his lap. This time the anticipation was mixed with apprehension.

Her brother-in-law indicated a row of empty seats and she moved into it. He positioned her in the middle of the row. He sat directly behind her.

On the screen, a naked man climbed upon the naked woman and began to simulate sex.

Within a minute someone had taken a seat at the end of the row in which she sat. She continued watching the screen. The man moved and took the seat next to her on the right.

Bianca watched the screen but the shapes were not real and the sex was not real. The fingers that touched her leg were real.

She was sitting with her legs crossed and the man

had put his left hand beneath the overhang of her skirt. The hand rested on the seat and the back of his fingers touched the nylon of her stocking.

Bianca kept her hands in her lap and didn't move. She tried to look sideways without making it obvious and got the impression that the man was also staring straight ahead at the screen. He was sitting with both feet flat on the floor and his legs slightly parted, his right hand in his lap.

The man moved his hand until the back of the fingers had crossed the welt of the stocking top and were touching the flesh of her thigh.

Both of them remained immobile for a minute and then, emboldened, the man traced with the back of his fingers the length of her right leg down to the knee. He covered her knee with his palm before moving it upwards again, on top of her leg, taking the skirt with it.

His hand crossed the welt of the stocking top again and ran along the front strap of the garter belt, all the way to her groin. It rested there a while, feeling the flesh, gauging the moment, before the fingers moved over the rise of her thigh and attempted to dip between her legs.

It was an impossible manoeuvre with her legs crossed but his fingers stroked her groin through the panties. She uncrossed her legs.

The man let out a sigh he seemed to have been holding for ever and turned in his seat. She was aware of him staring down at her legs, and he replaced his left hand with his right to stroke the inside of her thighs and move them open even more. His fingers moved now beneath the wide leg of the silk panties, delved in her pubic hair and hooked down into the groove that led to her vagina.

Bianca changed the position of her hips to give him access and a finger pushed inside her and she gasped at the lewdness of the situation and kept staring at the screen.

He now had two fingers inside her that he was moving without regard to her pleasure but for his own, to display his dominance.

In the periphery of her vision, she was aware of someone else moving down the row and taking the seat to her left.

The first man removed the fingers and put them in his mouth. He sucked them greedily before opening his trousers. Now the second man touched her, probing beneath the panties to find the wetness, before stroking her thighs and legs. She saw his hands; he was a negro.

She could smell the first man now he had released his erection. He took her right hand and placed it around its base and she began to masturbate him, while he unbuttoned her blouson and discovered her naked breasts. He leaned forward and sucked one into his mouth and slobbered at her nipple.

The black man had a finger inside her and was also rubbing her clitoris with his thumb and she felt her hips respond. She was very wet.

She also noticed other people sitting in the row in front. The other occupants of the auditorium had changed their seats but were not looking at the screen: their silhouettes were all watching what the two men were doing to her.

Bianca concentrated on making the white man reach his orgasm with her hand but he wanted more than that. He stopped sucking her breast and pulled her shoulders round and she closed her eyes. She didn't want to see him and she didn't want to kiss him. He pushed her down and she went towards the smell in the darkness and took his prick into her mouth.

What they were doing was dirty and disgusting but

his groan made her own juices run and she didn't object when the black man moved her from the seat. Her skirt was raised and she felt his fingers pushing the panties to one side and opening her vagina. He pushed his prick inside her in one full movement and now she groaned as well.

Bianca was uncomfortable and her senses were ragged. She had one knee on the seat in which she had been sitting, one foot on the floor, and was being held up by the black man's prick and his hands on her hips.

The white man moaned and jerked and held both her breasts in his hands. He squeezed them so hard when he came that she yelled and some of his sperm ran out of her mouth and down her chin. Behind her, the black man came, too. He held himself deep inside her as he pumped out his juices.

When he had finished, he helped her back into her seat and she sat, stunned and disorientated, her skirt around her waist, her blouson open and hanging off one shoulder to expose a breast.

The white man had gone but the black man remained in the seat next to her. Four silhouettes stared at her body. From one of them, a hand reached out.

Cosmo said: 'No. It's time to go. Come Bianca.'

She got unsteadily to her feet. The black man stood up and helped guide her along the row. As she passed one of the silhouettes, a hand went beneath her skirt and felt her buttocks but no one stopped her.

When she reached the aisle, Cosmo took over from the black man and led her out of the auditorium into the corridor that served all three theatres. He returned her handbag and she went into the ladies lavatory.

It smelled and was not particularly clean but she was grateful for its privacy. Her blouson was still open and the saliva from the white man still covered her right breast. Her nipples were hard and erect.

She buttoned herself up, rinsed her mouth with tap water and wiped it with a tissue before re-applying lipstick. She added a touch of perfume and took several deep breaths.

Bianca was disturbed but aroused and she hadn't orgasmed.

Cosmo was waiting and escorted her outside into the sunshine. People walked by them, going about their ordinary business. How many of these housewives or shop girls had been fucked in a cinema, she wondered?

Her brother-in-law again gave her a metro ticket and went his own way and she walked to the station in a daze. The young man was waiting. She held up the metro ticket and let it drop from her fingers. He turned and walked away and she followed.

The young man took the same street as the day before but walked past the turning that led to the derelict house. He turned into an alley fifty yards further on. Bianca stopped at the entrance. He unlocked a door and looked back towards her. It was an invitation. She walked past him and went through the door.

It led straight onto a flight of stairs. She went up them and the young man followed. She paused on the carpeted landing when faced with three doors, and he moved past her and pushed one of them open.

Bianca went into the young man's room. Posters of Gaugin were pinned to the walls, huge vibrant patches of colour. Books were stacked on the floor. A single bed with a clean yellow coverlet was by a window that looked out at a brick wall. There was a table and a chair. On the table were pencils, a tin that held pieces of charcoal, a box of pastel chalks and a sketch pad. Other sketches protruded from a folder that was propped in a corner.

He closed the door behind her but she didn't turn.

Bianca dropped her handbag on the floor, unbuttoned the blouson, removed it and placed it over tho back of the chair. She unzipped the skirt and stepped out of it, folded it and placed it on the seat of the chair. She removed the panties and left them on the floor, unfastened the garter belt and pushed the stockings from her legs while they were still attached to it. They, too, remained on the floor. She lay on her back on the bed and looked at him.

The young man hadn't moved. He still wore the jeans and the black leather jacket. His features were even but nondescript, as if he might grow into good looks with maturity. His hair was dark and thick. His eyes were soft and amber.

He walked to the side of the bed and picked up the panties, garter belt and stockings. He straightened them with care and placed them on top of the skirt on the chair.

Perhaps he's playing for time, Bianca thought. I've broken the rules and he doesn't know what to do.

The young man went back to the door, took off the jacket and hung it on a hook. Now he faced her, his eyes caressing her body. She responded and stretched. He pulled off his sweatshirt and his shoes and removed his jeans. The only thing he kept on were white boxer shorts.

It was Bianca's turn to caress him with her eyes. Strong legs, flat stomach, slim waist, a youthful upper torso that was masculine without being musclebound. It was the sort of body Michel would have had as a young man.

Their eyes met, properly, for the first time. Bianca made hers receptive. His held desire and something more but she couldn't tell what.

He moved to the bed and knelt by the side of it. His eyes moved over her body as intimately as the Blind Man's touch. He picked up her hand from the bed and put it to his lips and kissed each fingertip; his tongue licked down the inside of each finger and he kissed her palm open-mouthed.

The young man replaced her hand on the coverlet and went to the bottom of the bed. He did the same with her feet as he had with her hand, kissing and caressing them. His mouth moved along her legs to her knees. Now he climbed onto the bed, but lay on his stomach alongside her, not touching her with his body.

He kissed her arm and her shoulder and her neck and Bianca moaned gently and closed her eyes. His tongue flicked inside her ear and made love to it and she bit her bottom lip. His lips followed the line of her jaw round to her chin and, as she arched her head backwards, he licked down the inner curve of her throat all the way to her bosom.

The young man held himself above her, his body still not touching, as his mouth went over her right breast to suckle at her nipple. When it was wet, he gently rubbed his face against it before moving to her left breast and repeating the process.

Bianca remained passive but her body made wanting movements on the bed. Now she could feel his breath above her face with a hint of peppermint. His lips touched hers; they simply touched, waiting for an invitation.

She parted her lips and, in doing so, parted his. Her tongue slid between them and into his mouth. He maintained his immobility for only a second and then his mouth moved against hers and his tongue found hers and the kiss was deep and long. Her arms went around his neck and he finally lowered his body against her.

They touched each other, slowly exploring, and his gentleness aroused and frustrated her. He still wore the shorts and she slipped her hand inside through the opening at the front and found his erection hard and pulsing.

Perhaps he had kept the shorts on to stop himself from coming too soon?

She caressed it in her palm and he groaned and arched away. Her touch was too sensitive and she removed her hand but pushed at the waist band of the shorts. He sat on the edge of the bed and removed them and when he turned to face her again she opened her legs and guided him with her hands.

'Please,' she said.

He knelt between her thighs and she held herself open. He placed it at the mouth of her vagina and his eyelids began to tremble. She reached for his waist and pulled him into her fiercely and he fell against her, already beginning to twitch. He covered her mouth with his and she took his groan into her throat as he bucked and heaved and came inside her and her orgasm rose to meet him and they exchanged dying breaths.

When their senses returned, they stroked each other's faces, and she sensed his sexual renewal when his fingers moved from her sweat-streaked hair to her breasts. Now it was her turn to be gentle with him and she lay him on his back and began moving down his body.

They stayed in his room making love, dozing and making love, until it got dark. They murmured words to each other that neither understood but which they accepted with smiles, touches and kisses.

At last, Bianca got dressed and he watched with anxious eyes. She smiled at him and took a pencil and a piece of paper from the table and wrote on it the same time they had met each afternoon. She showed him the time and pointed at the floor and held her hands out to indicate the room.

'Here,' she said. 'Tomorrow.'

He understood and nodded and also dressed and

took her back towards the station but instead of a train, she pointed at the taxi rank.

The young man put her in a taxi and instructed the driver where to take her, and then hesitated, with the rear door of the taxi still open.

Bianca pulled him to her by the collar of the leather jacket and kissed him.

'Tomorrow,' she said.

'Tomorrow,' he repeated, mimicking the word and guessing at its meaning.

Chapter 12

Cosmo telephoned Bianca at the hotel the next day before he collected her and told her to wear the black dress they had bought two days before.

It buttoned down the front to the waist and had a scooped neckline that showed the swell of her breasts. She wore a half-cup black lace brassiere to enhance their appearance, black underwear and black stockings. When she inspected herself in the mirror, her reflection reminded her of how she had looked at her uncle's funeral.

The Doctor approved of the dress and took his seat and she sank comfortably onto the couch and stared at the patch of ceiling that had been witness to her past.

He said: 'Let us talk again about your relationship with your husband. Is it correct to say that he turned fantasy into reality?'

'Yes, I suppose he did.'

'You and your husband acted out scenes from your past: what you did with your uncle, what happened in the garden hut. Is that correct?'

'Yes.'

'You told him everything that you had experienced and he recreated it.'

'That's right.'

'Why?'

'Because he was jealous of what I had done without him and wanted to be part of it. Because he enjoyed the jealousy. To him, jealousy was an aphrodisiac.'

'Did you also tell him your fantasies?'

'Yes.'

'Did he turn those into reality, also?'

'Yes.'

'Tell me a fantasy that became a reality?'

Bianca smiled.

'I had told Michel about the boy who took me to the secret place in the fields and how his three friends watched us. In my fantasy, the three friends didn't stay in the woods.'

'And this became reality?'

'It happened in England. My husband had business in London and I went with him. After he had completed his business, we hired a car and drove into the country for a few days vacation. It was June and the weather was warm.

'We were near the coast and had driven past the gates of a boarding school, the sort of establishment where the English upper classes send their sons to be taught sodomy and nobility. We parked the car and followed a path through a wood. Our intention was to reach the coast to look at the scenery, enjoy the countryside and find a secluded place for sex.'

She had worn a pink *crêpe de chine* dress. The bodice was buttoned down the front to the waist, the skirt was loose and full.

'The path led us through a wood to the edge of the school's grounds. Boys of sixteen or seventeen were playing the English game of cricket. They wore white shirts and trousers. They were young and vibrant and full of life.

'Other youths lay on the grass nearby watching the game. They, too, wore white shirts and trousers, and blazers that were striped in red, black and gold. They were languid and talked to each other lazily, as if waiting for the day when they would be called upon to become their nation's bankers, lawyers and politicians. They had that infuriating English air of unruffled superiority.

'They stopped talking to stare at me as we walked into view. My breasts moved freely beneath the flimsy material and the skirt was thin enough to give hints of what was beneath. The superiority changed to longing.'

They were healthy young males who had attained the age of sexual freedom but who were caught in the constraints of a public school system that denied their needs. They might as well have been in prison without access to female company.

Bianca felt the force of their frustrations and pent-up urges in their hungry gaze. No wonder they were rumoured to sublimate their real desires with each other in sodomy. She knew that she embodied all that they might wish for, that she was the fantasy they had all dreamed of touching, holding, fucking.

As they walked past, Michel stroked her buttocks with a possessive hand and whispered to her: 'Tonight you will be the cause of the spilling of a gallon of sperm. They are drinking in your memory for their own furtive sex. When they masturbate beneath the sheets they will be thinking of you.'

Being the cause of such an effect was thrilling. Her eyes sparkled as she saw the lust in their eyes.

'The path went back into the wood and we both knew some of the boys would follow, that their desires would lead them to hope they might see something more, or simply to keep in sight the fantasy I had become to them. We paused a little way into the trees while we kissed and touched each other and saw that four of them had, indeed, begun to follow.

'We went further into the wood and they maintained a discreet distance, stopping when we did, hiding in the foliage or behind trees, to keep their desires secret.

Eventually we came to a clearing that suited all our purposes.'

The grass was a soft, verdant, virginal stage, the sun provided a dappled spotlight and the remnants of a shattered tree was their only scenery. Its slim trunk had been stripped of bark and was luminescent and smooth. It rose from the ground angled like a healthy erection. Two dead branches, equally white and smooth, split apart at the height of Bianca's shoulders.

The Doctor said: 'What purposes?'

'We put on a show for the four boys who had hidden to watch us.'

Michel placed her against the tree and they kissed. He unfastened her bodice of the dress and she released her arms from the sleeves so that the material hung around her waist. As he licked her nipples, he raised her skirt and his hands roamed her flesh, delved between her legs, his fingers entered her vagina.

She imagined the four youths who were watching, imagined what they were thinking, what they were doing. Her eyes were closed, her arms spread along the two branches, holding on to them as the feeling of danger and desire filled the pit of her stomach.

Bianca said: 'I displayed my body. I fellated my husband and we had sex. And all the time the four boys watched.'

Michel leaned against the tree and she knelt before him on the grass, her tongue moving over her lips in anticipation, her nipples erect and her breasts trembling. She unfastened his trousers and took out his erection and rolled her face against it, brushing it with her hair, letting it slide over her features and along her neck. and all the time she watched the woods to discover where their watchers lurked.

Two of them were to her left, a third to her right but she couldn't locate the fourth youth. She could, however, hear their surreptitious moans and the rustle of clothing and undergrowth.

Bianca at last guided Michel's prick into her mouth and was rewarded with an audible groan from her left. She fellated it expertly, noisily and with relish, and elicited deep groans from her husband. He took her head in both his hands and, to fulfil another adolescent fantasy, he held it firmly whilst he fucked her mouth.

When she got back to her feet they kissed deeply, passionately, exchanging messages with their eyes. He turned her and she faced the tree and spread her arms again as she looked over it, and down into the face of the fourth youth.

Michel raised her dress at the back and she opened her legs. He entered her from behind, sliding into her wetness with ease. She continued to stare into the shocked face of the fair-haired boy as she moaned.

Her husband fucked her and she raised the skirt of her dress at the front so that the youth would have an unrestricted view. His mouth remained open. He was still surprised at being discovered and unsure what he should do. Bianca's expression and her moans, and her gesture in raising her skirt, reassured him. His gaze dropped from her face to her body and he resumed his masturbation.

Michel orgasmed, his hips heaving against her buttocks in his spasm, shouting out his pleasure. Bianca shouted with him and stared into the eyes of the youth as he came as well, his mouth open, his eyes protruding, a vein throbbing in his forehead as the vein had throbbed in her boyfriend's prick all those years before.

Bianca didn't come. She was primed and she was ready but she was saving the moment for a development she couldn't anticipate. The excitement, the danger, the power filled her.

The Doctor said: 'What happened after you and Michel had finished your . . . demonstration?'

'Michel invited them out of hiding. He invited them to touch their fantasy.'

Her husband stepped away and fastened his clothes and she remained in the same position although she allowed the skirt of her dress to drop back into place. He now spoke loudly in English to their watchers. Not understanding what he was telling them was an added excitement. Now she almost did come at the thought of the possibilities.

Michel spoke again, reassuringly, and the boy in front of her rose from his hiding place, pushing his prick back into his clothes. He was tall and lithe. He stepped forward into the clearing and she turned round to see the others appearing from their hiding places, their clothes hastily fastened: a small youth with dark complexion, a plump youth, a freckle-faced youth with a shock of red hair.

The atmosphere was heavy as if a storm might break at any moment; Bianca felt as if she were the storm.

A while ago, the youths had been languid with superiority. It had been replaced by dishevelment, embarrassment and longing. As Michel spoke to them, their expressions changed again, to disbelief, amazement and, finally, to become heavy with lustful anticipation.

Michel held out his hand to her and she joined him in the dappled sunlight on the grass. He kissed her and whispered one word into her mouth.

'Enjoy,' he said.

He stepped back and spoke to the boys, totally in command and they willing to be commanded. The four of them approached her, tentative, still unsure. They surrounded her, their breath shallow and ragged, the plump one holding his trousers up with one hand and casting a look to Michel for confirmation that they had understood correctly.

Her husband spoke again, softly, encouragingly.

The tall fair-haired boy was the first to reach out a

hand. He stroked the curve of Bianca's left buttock through the thin material of the dress. When she moved against his hand, his touch became firmer. His hand began to feel her flesh greedily and she felt the selfishness begin to assert itself.

Emboldened by what they saw, the others reached out, touching her naked breasts, her thighs, her buttocks. The fair-haired boy led the way again by sliding the dress upwards until he touched the nakedness above the stockings.

Bianca was dizzy with sex. It showed on her face and the boys recognised that her expression mirrored their own. They wanted to possess her as they had wanted to possess the bodies of the women in the magazines they sneaked into school. They wanted to possess her as the boys who had hidden in the wood and masturbated had wanted to possess her all those years before.

Her dress was around her waist, fingers clumsily explored her vagina but she was so wet they didn't hurt; hands groped her buttocks beneath the loose panties. The small youth suckled on a breast, a hand gripped the other breast fiercely as if it wanted it as a trophy.

They pressed against her, tongues licking her neck, her shoulders, her breasts; hands inside her panties and fingers inside her. Their breath was hot, their hands sweating, they gasped loudly when their mouths left her flesh.

The first orgasm took her and she could have swooned but the hands held her upright. She came again, and again, and again.

A naked penis was against her leg, partly on her stocking, partly on her skin, pointing upwards alongside a strap of the garter belt. No sooner had it touched her than it came, spurting wetness onto her thigh. She saw the face of the plump boy contorting at the release and he sagged away, his trousers round his knees.

From a million miles away, she heard Michel's voice. He shouted again and the boys released her.

In Italian, Michel said: 'Choose one.'

Bianca pointed to the small dark youth.

Michel spoke to the boy in English and then to her in Italian.

He said: 'Your mouth, Bianca.'

The boy came forward hesitantly and she knelt on the grass and held her arms out to him. He was nervous at being selected but he allowed her to pull him closer and to begin to unfasten his trousers. As she started to open them, his resolve again threatened to break, but she persisted.

Bianca pulled down the white flannels and saw the reason for his concern. He had come in his trousers and his white cotton underpants were stuck to his genitals with the sperm.

She smiled up into his face and licked her lips as she peeled down the underpants. His erection was as nervous as he was and he shook with fright when she took hold of it. She moved her fingers firmly around its base and it began to stiffen and, as she guided it to her lips, she saw that his two companions had opened their clothes and were now openly masturbating while they watched.

The erection was a respectable size for a youth so small, slim but long and uncircumcised. She slid back the foreskin with her lips as she sucked it into her mouth and he cried in pleasure and continued to cry whilst she sucked him swiftly to a conclusion. His spurts were accompanied by yelps as his fantasy was fulfilled.

He staggered a few paces away before sinking to the ground. The other two youths continued masturbating and she remained kneeling on the grass.

She heard Michel's voice through a haze, as if he were directing from another world, as he instructed them in English. They stepped closer, their shortening breaths announcing their imminent orgasms, and discharged themselves upon her breasts.

The Doctor said: 'Did they have sex with you, Bianca?'

'No. They were allowed to touch and they were allowed to look. I fellated one of them: a small dark-skinned youth who looked as I imagined Michel might have looked at the same age.'

'Did they come?'

'Oh yes.'

'And you enjoyed watching them?'

'Yes.'

'Michel was in control of everything that happened?'

'Yes.'

'Were you disappointed that you did not have complete sex with the young men?'

'No. That had not been part of my fantasy. My fantasy was to arouse them so much that they lost control, that they were reduced to masturbating in public. In my fantasy I gave them part of what they wanted whilst withholding the ultimate gift that they hoped I might bestow. In my fantasy their male superiority was left in shreds.'

'Wasn't there a danger that they might have stolen that ultimate gift?'

'The danger was intentional, another aphrodisiac. But these were English public-schoolboys, bred on discipline. They accepted Michel's authority without question. They were perfect pawns.'

Afterwards, Michel helped her put on the bodice of the dress, and led her from the woods. The material stuck to her skin with the juices she had elicited from the young male bodies.

They drove to a hotel where Michel booked a room

and they spent the rest of the afternoon making love and having sex, Bianca relinquishing the dress slowly, so they could smell the young men, so they could rejuvenate the congealing sperm with their sweat.

The Doctor said: 'You have explained how Michel was a voyeur in the garden hut, a stage-manager when you were with the English schoolboys, and how he left you alone with the boy at the hotel. Did he also participate when he shared you with other people?'

'Of course.'

'Give me an example.'

Chapter 13

Bianca remembered the villa again, that long hot summer.

'Yesterday I told you about the villa and the English girl.'

'Yes.'

'The English girls went home and two days later, it was time for the Norwegians also to leave. On their last night, we had a farewell dinner. We met them at a night club in the town. They and Michel wore shirts and slacks. I wore a thin blue dress, white underwear at Michel's suggestion, because it looked so good against my tan; stockings and high heels. I had coiffured my hair and wore make-up and jewellery. It was the first time they had seen me with clothes on. They were even more interested in my body now that it was hidden.

'We dined and we danced. It was not disco music, it was music meant for dancing. Mood music with the lights low. The three men took turns in partnering me on the floor. Michel danced with me first and held my body close and I could feel his erection in his trousers. His right hand stroked my buttocks through the thin dress.

'The brothers were uncomfortable at first, at holding me in their arms. Seeing my body at a distance was different to holding it close. I put them at their ease by being natural and moving against them. They moved closer in response. They both had erections.

'They became impatient when they had to wait for

their turn to dance and, the next time, they too touched my buttocks and my legs through the dress, when they had their backs to Michel so that he wouldn't notice.

'Eventually, Michel suggested we go back to the villa for a last drink. He drove and I sat in the back of the car with our two guests. I sat in the middle and their thighs pressed against mine. I held their hands in their laps so that I could feel their pricks.

'The journey wasn't long and, just before we got there, I turned to the one on my left, touched his face with my hand and kissed him – an exploratory kiss with my tongue in his mouth. He was startled for a second, then his hand went to my breasts. His brother was touching my legs on top of the dress. I then turned to the other one and kissed him in the same way. He, too, felt my breasts while the first, emboldened by the intimate contact, slipped a hand beneath my skirt and touched my leg above the stocking.'

She smiled.

'Men are always fascinated by that area of nakedness above a stocking.

'Then we were at the villa. I was tingling at what might happen next. We went into the lounge and Michel played soft music on the tape deck. He didn't put on any lights, he didn't want to spoil the moonlight that shone from the ocean through the open french windows. We drank champagne and he danced with me again while the brothers watched.

'We moved slowly to the music and kissed slowly, his hips moving against mine, his hands opening the front of my dress to feel my naked breasts. I was aroused and didn't try to disguise the fact. I made noises when he touched and kissed me.

'The music stopped and Michel stepped away and said something to one of the Norwegians. The man put down his glass and, when the music started again, he took me in his arms and we danced. His erection was huge against my thigh and when I kissed him I felt him shake with desire. One of his hands went inside my dress and held a breast and I rubbed myself against his thigh. I could have made him come just by swaying against him but I resisted and the song finished.

'His brother took his place for the next track and we repeated the process. Our mouths met, his hand went inside my dress, his erection pressed against me. This time I moved my hips and stood open-legged against him, so that his prick pressed against my stomach as I swayed to the music.

'Michel came to stand behind me and I felt his erection in the groove between my buttocks. The three of us moved together, the Norwegian kissing my mouth, Michel kissing my neck, the two pricks rubbing slowly.

'Then Michel slipped the dress from my shoulders and I pulled my arms free and put them back round the Norwegian's neck. I was naked to the waist and his hands held both my breasts. Michel raised the skirt of my dress at the back, lifting it to my hips, his hands in my panties and on my buttocks. He put a hand between my legs and felt me open and felt the wetness inside.

'He stepped away and the second Norwegian came forward and took my husband's place. The brothers kissed me and touched me, feeling my body with greedy hands, their erections solid inside their trousers, their fingers pushing inside me and making me wetter still.

'I looked away from them as they licked my neck and my breasts and saw Michel drinking champagne, watching. Then he put down the glass and removed all his clothes.

'Michel took me from the two men and led me to the bedroom. They followed. He unfastened the dress at the waist and it fell to the floor and he lay me on the bed. He got onto the bed with me and we kissed and touched. He suckled my nipples, stroked me between my legs, pushed off the panties and covered my vagina with his mouth. I was bucking and moaning but my eyes were wide open as I watched the blonde brothers watching us.

'My husband raised his head and whispered along the length of my body. He said, come for them. Then he dipped his head again and his tongue went inside me and it was as if I had been given permission and I squirmed and moaned and came.'

Bianca paused, enjoying the memory.

The Doctor said: 'What did the men do?'

'They stripped naked and climbed on the bed.'

'What did they do?'

She smiled.

'Everything.'

'Tell me.'

'Michel entered me first. He held himself above me on his arms while he pushed in and out. The brothers lay one on either side, their hands on my breasts and my thighs. Then Michel moved away and the brothers had me in turn. They both came very quickly, lying on top of me, face to face. Too quickly for me to come.

'They rested alongside us, whilst Michel moved me about the bed, putting it in my mouth, taking me from behind, sitting me astride him. I came like that because the two men were again aroused. They lay masturbating whilst they watched us. It released my inhibitions and I came. After that, I didn't stop coming.

'They wanted to do everything to me. I was turned over and sucked one prick whilst another entered my vagina from behind. I was moved into positions, sat upon erections. The pricks were interchangeable. After a while, I couldn't even tell which was Michel's. Our bodies were soaked in sweat and juices, the smell was glorious. I lost count of the number of times I came.

'Towards the end, I was aware that Michel was manoeuvring the brothers. I lay upon one, my legs across his hips, his prick inside my vagina. The other lay near my head and I sucked him. Behind me, Michel licked me between my buttocks, pushing his tongue into my anus. It made me contract with pleasure. Then he pushed his finger inside and I knew what was coming next.

'He knelt behind me. My anus was wet and I relaxed it to allow him entry. He pushed inside and his groan echoed round the room. The brothers paused. He didn't move his prick, but held it there, until I adjusted to it. Then he pushed, groaning again because it was so tight, and the brothers took it as their cue and continued, but more frantically now that they were aware of what was happening, that I had accepted all three at once.

'We didn't all come together. Michel came first, yelling and shaking as if in a fit. That caused the prick inside my vagina to explode. When he had finished, his brother moved from my mouth, lay me on my back and took me again from the front, staring down at me with wide eyes, almost in wonder, as he pumped into me. The other Norwegian was drained, discarded, and Michel lay, open-mouthed in exhaustion, watching. He gripped my hand and I came, screaming, and the blond Norwegian came, lifting my hips off the mattress with his orgasm.'

The silence stretched and Bianca had no reason to disturb it. She moved her thighs together.

The Doctor's voice was muted.

'What were your feelings when it was happening?'

'There were no specific feelings, apart from the pain when Michel first entered my anus. But the pain melted into the pleasure. If there was any feeling at all, it was of sex. Of heightened pleasure that was beyond the bounds of normality. Total sex, total use, total abuse, total pleasure.

'For two or three hours, we had built the expectancy like foreplay. The clothes I wore, the looks at dinner where I was conscious of how I used my mouth to eat, dancing at the club, the atmosphere of lust in the car, everything had built gradually, excitingly, tinglingly, towards what amounted to an orgasm that went on for perhaps three hours.'

'Afterwards, did you feel guilty about what happened?'

'No.'

'Did you regret what happened?'

'No. I liked the brothers. They were handsome, clean, polite and they went back to Norway the next morning. It was perfectly arranged.'

'So it's best to have sex with strangers?'

'Of course.'

'Why?'

'If you have sex with a friend there is always the chance it might develop into something more, even if you don't want it to and don't encourage it to. The friend could make demands or think he had fallen in love. It's safer with a stranger.'

'Is it also safer when someone else arranges it for you? Like your husband? Like me?'

'It can be more convenient, but I have arranged my own encounters, without Michel. We agreed we could do that as long as I remembered every detail to tell him so he could be jealous and we could re-enact the scene.'

The Doctor said: 'With the girl in the villa, you at one stage took the initiative. But have you otherwise always been passive in your sexual encounters?'

She smiled.

'Most of the time, men like to believe they are dominant. I allow them to believe that they are. But I know that it is me who has aroused them. That is not being passive. It is my decision to allow them to do things to me but I could also stop things happening at any time.'

The Doctor said: 'On occasions, you might not be able to stop things happening. If you tried, it might turn into rape.'

'There is that possibility,' Bianca said. 'But it's a possibility that every woman has to live with, whether they are sexually active or walking through a park. Besides, rape is an act of violence not an act of sexuality. In the situations I have instigated, I don't think I have ever been in danger of rape.'

The Doctor sighed.

'I think, Bianca, that we have perhaps almost come to the end of the talking. Cosmo will take you on one final pilgrimage. Tomorrow's visit here could be your last. I believe you have made great progress. Do you agree?'

Bianca thought of the young man.

'Yes. I agree.'

'Good. Then I'll leave you a moment while I have a word with your brother-in-law. And I look forward to tomorrow.' She could tell from the tone of his voice that he was smiling. 'You said your first year of marriage was a graduation. Tomorrow you will graduate again.'

Chapter 14

The church was hidden in a forgotten square that had been isolated by an arterial road. The small graveyard was overgrown and its stones were crumbling and in disrepair.

Cosmo took her to the vestry door. It was unlocked and they went inside. The room was musty, the stained glass windows high in the thick stone walls were dirty; some were broken. The only furniture was a church bench.

She waited in the room while her brother-in-law went into the church. He didn't return but a cleric did, a rotund priest in a black cassock. Below its hem, Bianca noticed his bare ankles and bare feet in sandals.

He smiled at her and indicated the open door that led into the church tower.

'The view is invigorating,' he said, in Italian.

Bianca went through the door and began to climb. The steps were stone, steep and wound around inside the tower. She realised that the cleric, who was some paces behind, would be able to see straight up her skirt.

She paused and looked down. He was staring upwards, red faced and panting and she didn't know whether it was from the climb or the view. He had said it was invigorating.

Cosmo had chosen the dress well. The knee-length skirt was full and hung away from her legs. The man below would be able to see the black stockings and garter-belt straps, the white flesh, the folds of the black silk panties, and the shadows that they hid.

Bianca paused again at a window in the tower, almost at the top. She spread her legs, as if balancing to get a better view. If this was what he wanted, she would make it worth the climb.

At the top, she looked out over the suburb of the city, spoiled by the main road to the east, reconstruction dusting the skyline to the south, the river to the west. She stared towards the north, and tried to work out where the young man's apartment might be.

Behind her, the cleric leaned against her, pointing to landmarks, and explaining them. The explanations were as mundane as the sights but she understood his words. She also understood his body. She could feel his stiffness through the cassock and her dress.

At last he got to the point and said: 'I believe, my dear, that you are a sinner. That you have led a lascivious life.'

'Yes, Father.'

He moved his hips and his erection pushed against her buttocks.

'I am told you have known many men, and even women, in the deepest sexual sense.'

'That is true.'

He put his arms either side of her, trapping her against the parapet, his hands gripping the stonework.

'And that you regret nothing but have gloried in sex and passion.'

'I regret nothing.'

His face moved close to her hair and she could smell a discreet aftershave.

'And the sex?'

'The sex was glorious. Sex freely given and taken is glorious. I regret nothing.'

He pressed against her and whispered in her ear.

'Will you ever stop sinning?'

'Sex isn't sinful. It can be as pure as love. As pure as an orgasm.'

He shuddered, and now his whole body was against her.

'If I were to offer you the city before you, a kingdom for you to rule, would you forsake sex?'

'Never. Sexual desire is as natural as birth and death. I will never forsake sex. If I become too old to practise it with my body, I will still enjoy it in my mind. I will wallow in my memories, and I have plenty of memories.'

His mouth was at her ear, his lips touching that organ's sensitive lobes, the words were soft but urgent:

'If I were to promise you the whole world, would you forsake sex?'

'The whole world is sex. That is the only reality. That is why men fight wars, desire power, build houses.' She smiled into the breeze, beginning to respond to the absurdity of the pantomime in which she was prime player. 'Fucking makes the world go round.'

He groaned when she said fucking and pressed his erection hard against her buttocks.

'Have you been with many men, my child?'

He kept pushing.

'Many.'

'And have you always been a willing partner?'

'No.'

'You were forced?'

'No.'

'I don't understand. If you were not willing and you were not forced . . .?'

'The only absolutes in life are birth and death, in between there are shadows. Sex is life. There are no absolutes in sex, either. Sometimes, the sex is unexpected, inappropriate. Sometimes it emerges from a situation like a serpent, catching you unawares, leaving you defenceless when you didn't realise you would need defences. It is easy for it to happen when a woman is neither willing nor opposed.'

Bianca's exposition had cooled the cleric's ardour, but only slightly.

'I think it's time we went down,' he said. 'You will confess to me how you were unwilling and yet not forced.'

He began to descend and she followed. He frequently paused and looked up, into her face and into her skirt. When they regained the vestry, he sat on the bench and dropped a cushion on the floor at his feet.

'Kneel, child.'

Bianca knelt on the cushion between his open legs. She was aware that he was staring intently at her bosom in the low-cut dress. This was her last assignment and she would complete the course.

She said: 'Forgive me, Father, for I have sinned.'

'Your life has been full of sin, my child. Tell me about the incident of which we spoke.'

'It was six months after my husband died. I was twenty-six years old and had inherited an international company. Two of my husband's closest colleagues took me to dinner. One was an accountant, the other was chief designer. They were solicitous at dinner, but they gave me too much wine. They also talked business, but they talked down to me because I was a woman and because I was twenty-six. They were mapping out a future for themselves in the company which my husband had built and which was now mine.'

The cleric held Bianca's shoulders and moved her bosom against his erection.

'Go on, my child.'

'After dinner, they took me to a suite in the hotel and gave me more wine. I thought their plans for the future were foolish but didn't tell them. I still thought they were entertaining me because they had regard for me, and because I was my husband's widow. In the suite, I sensed the atmosphere change.'

Now the cleric groaned in anticipation and moved his erection against the cushion of her breasts.

'What did they do?'

'I had become melancholy as well as intoxicated with the wine and the accountant held me in his arms. It was a comfort and I relaxed against him, a comfort to feel a man's body next to mine after losing my husband. At that time, I didn't believe it would lead to anything else.'

The cleric was moving rhythmically.

'Go on,' he said.

'He suggested I lay down for a while, and I let him lead me to the bedroom and I lay upon the bed and fell asleep. I don't know how much later it was, but when I awoke I was being kissed and, in my dreams it had felt good, and I was kissing back. My mouth was open, my tongue was demanding, and a thigh was between my legs.

'My senses came back slowly as my dress was pushed up and hands went between my legs. The mouth that had been covering mine had now descended to suck upon a breast that had been released. Both men were touching me, opening me, discovering me. I wanted to say no, to tell them to stop, but fingers were already inside me and the designer was talking in obscenities.

'I knew it had gone too far, and I thought that if there was blame then part of it might be mine, that I had, perhaps, unwittingly led them to believe that my body would be available to them. Perhaps they had thought my melancholy and tiredness had been a ploy to encourage them to take me.'

The cleric was groaning and rubbing but impatient with the pace of the confession.

'But what did they do?' he said.

'Afterwards, of course, I realised they had probably planned it all along, had engineered the situation from which I could not retreat. I was wearing, as always, the underwear my husband had encouraged me to wear, black lace and stockings that would entice any man, and my unconscious body had responded automatically when they had started their intimacies.'

'But what happened?'

Bianca was aware of the cleric's frustration and took pity on him, even though her own arousal was slight.

'They removed most of my clothes and most of their own, and they fucked me.'

'They did what?'

'They fucked me, Father.'

'How, my child?' His words were tight little sounds that escaped from a constricted throat. 'How did they fuck you, my child?'

'They fucked my vagina, they fucked my anus, they pushed their pricks between my breasts.' She opened the buttons at the top of the dress, freed her breasts and pressed them harder against him. 'And they fucked my mouth.'

The cleric gasped and pulled aside the cassock to reveal his own prick, sprouting from ginger curls beneath a fat belly. He pushed it between her globes and emulated what she had described.

His prick was hot, his belly was sweating and he was gasping for air like a marathon runner. Bianca began to enjoy and share his excitement because she was its cause and she controlled it.

'What did they do to your mouth, Bianca?'

He heaved and sweated.

'They fucked it, Father.'

He groaned.

'Show me, my child. Show me.'

Bianca dipped her head, took his prick into her mouth and sucked, whilst working the base of the shaft with her fingers. As he came, she gripped the base tight between forefinger and thumb to extend the orgasm and increase the pleasure.

His yells echoed around the dusty vestry but the only people he could disturb would be the dead outside in the graveyard.

Slowly, he subsided onto the bench, lying upon it sideways, his legs splayed, and the cassock open and the angry implement that had demanded so much attention already shrinking into a little boy's plaything.

Cosmo emerged from the church.

She stood up, fastened her dress and licked the sperm from the corners of her mouth.

'Do I get absolution, Father?'

The cleric raised a hand and waved but did not open his eyes.

Cosmo said: 'Time to go, Bianca.'

They walked into warm sunshine and a light breeze. As they approached the gate, she read a name and a date on a headstone. It told of a man named Petra who had died in 1827. She paused by the stone and calculated from the earlier date that he had been twenty-four when he had died.

What was the world like in 1827? Had Petra been married? Had he taken his sexual pleasure from the maid? Had he been racked by guilt at his erection in an age ruled by poverty and a mindless God? Had he been celibate and died a virgin, his only orgasm being death?

Bianca stroked the stone, fingering the worn upright grooves of the name, as if enticing an erection.

Whatever his marital condition, she had no doubt Petra's life would have been ruled by his prick: coveting his neighbour's wife, adultery, masturbation, guilt, praying for purity. Maybe he had died of syphilis?

Cosmo waited by the gate.

'Bianca?'

She joined him and they continued on their way.

She was happy to be led by Cosmo, through the sidestreets, back to the area of the suburb that she knew.

As they walked, she reflected on the role of the erection throughout time. Eve hadn't been seduced by an apple, but by the serpent that had arisen from between Satan's legs. The Spartans at the pass had fought for their country but also for their lovers. Priests had invented confession to cleanse their own souls because of the misdeeds of their own erections, whether physical or fantasised.

The prick, Bianca decided, had a lot to answer for. Particularly vulnerable were those men who equated pricks with power instead of passion, whose ego-erections ruled without intellect or imagination.

The night the accountant and the designer had used her in the hotel suite had not been rape, but it had been sex that had been instigated without her agreement. It had been dictated by ego-erections. To Bianca, the sex had been immaterial and, once it had started, she had not given them the satisfaction of attempting to stop it.

Instead, she had drained them and taken her satisfaction from their discomforture when their angry erections had shrunk to little boys' playthings that she had viewed with contempt.

What Bianca had taken exception to was their disloyalty to her late husband, their breaking of the trust she herself had placed in them and, in particular, for talking down to her about business because she was a twenty-six-year-old beautiful woman.

She gained further satisfaction by showing them she was a twenty-six-year-old beautiful woman with executive power: she had had them fired.

Sex was life, and life was sex. Sometimes it was simple, sometimes complicated by jealousies, guilt and relationships. Bianca had attempted to keep it simple since Michel had died but the last three days had given her a taste for more than uncomplicated sex.

Her body had been exposed to sensation and satiation, but the previous afternoon she had made love instead of sex. She was ready again to engage her emotions without a guide like Cosmo, and see where they led her.

But what if the young man was only playing a part to the Doctor's orders, as she had played her part?

Chapter 15

Bianca was early. The outer door was unlocked and she climbed the stairs to the young man's apartment. She knocked but there was no reply. The handle turned when she tried it and she stepped into the room that held the bed and the table. The young man wasn't there.

An opened bottle of red wine and a bottle of mineral water were on the table, with a glass and a folder of drawings. She used the glass that had already been used, and mixed red wine with the water to wash the taste of the cleric's sperm from her mouth.

She unfastened the dress and stepped out of it, dropping it across the chair, and enjoyed the feeling of liberating her body. She added more red wine to the glass and opened the folder.

The pictures were line drawings of a couple having sex. They were sectionalised drawings that never showed the couple completely, but which focused on different acts, different shapes, different parts of the body.

A giant phallus was being guided by a feminine hand into a feminine mouth. Spread thighs framed a vagina into which the owner had delicately inserted a finger. The same phallus strained between two full breasts.

The whole range of permutations were covered and, although the drawings were not brilliant pieces of work, they were effective.

Bianca looked back at the first one and thought

she recognised the girl with the open mouth. She definitely recognised the young man as the model in his own self-portraits, from his phallus and from the backs of his knees.

As a child, her first sexual stirrings had been aroused by looking at looking at the backs of boys' knees. She still enjoyed looking at strong male legs and holding them behind the knees with her palms.

Bianca wondered whether what she felt was jealousy or arousal, or whether there was any difference between the two. The difference was in possession. She and the young man had given of themselves to each other, but they had not entered into a bond of possession. Besides, the drawings had been done before they had met.

The outer door opened and closed and footsteps came up the stairs fast. She turned to face the apartment door, suddenly aware that, if it was a stranger who burst in upon her, she was provocatively undressed. It wasn't a stranger; it was the young man.

He stopped in the doorway in surprise and his eyes feasted upon her body. Then, without a word being spoken, he took her in his arms and they kissed. He was no longer shy or tentative; the surprise of her presence and her attire had aroused him and made him demanding. Bianca's arousal matched his instantaneously. She demanded, too.

The young man pushed her onto the bed and used his mouth between her legs and she came, sweetly, quickly, fiercely. He made her remain in the same position whilst he undressed; her body on the bed, her feet, still in high-heeled shoes, upon the floor. Now his mouth was tracing its way up her legs again and into the valley between her thighs. As he lapped between the lips of her vagina, he pushed her high-heeled feet between his legs and rubbed his erection against her ankles.

His mouth and his masturbation brought on another orgasm for Bianca and, as she recovered, he manoeuvred her feet again, pressing the soles of her shoes and heels against his abdomen, whilst his prick slid between the patent leather. She dug her heels into his flesh and he groaned, and she served him small portions of pain with the pleasure.

Bianca varied the position by putting one of her feet between his legs so that his prick lay against her nyloned ankle, the toe of the shoe digging towards his anus. With the other foot, she made steps around his abdomen and near the root of his erection, pressing with toe and heel to elicit ever louder moans.

Her hands were between her legs, three fingers of the left inside her, two fingers of the right rubbing at her clitoris.

The young man bucked at her feet, moaning with the pleasure, the pain and the sight of her own ministrations.

She lifted the free foot and removed the shoe. She put the shoe between her legs and pushed the toe into her vagina, groaning and lifting her hips to meet it. For a few seconds, she fucked herself with the shoe before removing it and offering the smeared leather of the toe to the young man.

As he fellated it, he came, his sperm shooting from her ankle to above her knee.

They rested but he was soon hard again, and they made love and had sex in all the positions he had drawn and more that Bianca introduced him to. When he orgasmed a second time, they were both tired and she fell into a light sleep.

When Bianca awoke she was alone in the bed. The young man was standing by the table, in his jeans, counting money in his hand. He looked at the almost empty bottles on the table and tapped a finger. She guessed he might be as hungry and thirsty as she was but did not have the money to buy supplies.

She stretched her hand and found her bag on the floor by the bed. He turned at the movement and she smiled. From the bag she took her purse and held out to him some notes. He began to shake his head but she looked him in the eye and asked without words, why not?

He smiled and shrugged and took the money, pointed to the wine and made a mime of putting food to his mouth and eating and she laughed. The young man finished dressing and left the apartment.

Bianca stretched again, feeling more complete than she had since her husband died. Not as complete, for her years with Michel would always be special, but more able to face the possibility of giving of herself rather than just her body.

She rolled onto her stomach and her hand touched the floorboards. Her fingers went beneath the bed and found a box. She pulled it out and lay on the mattress looking down at it. It was a cigar box.

Men kept secrets beneath the bed and Bianca had a twinge of conscience. If she lifted the lid would she be breaking a trust? Her curiosity told her that she wouldn't and that if the box contained secrets the young man hadn't wanted her to find, he would have hidden them better. She lifted the lid.

Inside were Polaroid photographs. Bianca lifted them out and looked through them. They were photographs from which the young man had created the drawings. Photographs of the young man and the woman whom she thought she had recognised. Now she did: it was the girl with whom he had been in the dress shop.

Jealousy or arousal?

She didn't care. The photographs made her horny and she touched herself between her legs as she looked at them. The door opened and the girl in the photographs stepped into the apartment.

The girl stopped in the open doorway; Bianca raised a thigh across her vagina in an automatic gesture of protection. The girl's gaze went from the Polaroid photograph in Bianca's left hand, down her body to where her right hand disappeared between her thighs.

Bianca lowered the protective thigh to reveal the exact location of her fingers, and turned the photograph towards her in explanation.

The girl closed the door behind her and said something in French.

Bianca said: 'I'm sorry. I don't understand.'

The girl raised her eyes and changed languages.

In Italian, she said: 'Who are you?'

'My name is Bianca.'

'Where is Paul?'

Paul. The young man suddenly had a name. He was no longer anonymous, he had a home and an identity as an artist.

'He went to buy wine and food.' Bianca absentmindedly removed the fingers from her vagina and put them to her mouth. She licked the tips delicately. 'Is Paul your lover?'

'No. He's my brother.'

Bianca dropped her eyes to the photograph she held that showed the young woman guiding Paul's prick into her mouth.

The young woman looked around the room, as if checking if anything else was out of place, as well as the photographs. She dropped her handbag on the table next to the folder of drawings.

She said: 'You have looked at these?'

'Yes.'

Bianca picked up all the photographs from the mattress and dropped them into the box, closed the lid and pushed it back beneath the bed, back into the place for secrets. She continued to lie on top of the sheets, naked but for her stockings and garter belt, unconcerned by the presence of Paul's sister, but curious.

'What's your name?' she said.

'Madeleine.'

When she had first seen the young man and the young woman in the dress shop, Bianca had thought them to be brother and sister. They had similar faces except that, while Paul's was waiting for maturity to make it handsome, Madeleine's was pretty with youth.

The girl wore a short cheesecloth dress, white ankle socks and flat shoes. Her legs and arms were tanned golden, her hair black, straight and shiny. Bianca wondered if she had attained such an erotic appearance by chance or design.

Bianca said: 'Who took the photographs?'

'Paul. The camera has a cable release.'

'He took the photographs to make the drawings?'

'Yes. He sells them to tourists.'

Bianca stared at Madeleine, so demure in white ankle socks, and tried to reconcile the reality with the image in the photographs.

Madeleine said: 'You want to know why?'

'Yes. I never had a brother. If I had, I don't know how I would have felt about him.'

'I love Paul because I am his sister, but I am not in love with him. The sex just happened. It was simply sex.'

Bianca said: 'I am in love with him, but I don't know him, therefore I don't love him. Do you see what I mean?'

Madeleine nodded.

'I think so.'

'I don't know how long being in love will last. I don't know whether Paul is in love with me because we cannot talk to each other with words. From his eyes, I think he is in love with me for now. We make love when we have sex. It's a long time since I made love. I'm very grateful to him.'

She sat up on the bed, patted the mattress and, after a moment's hesitation, Madeleine sat on the edge.

Bianca said: 'Tell me how the sex happened.'

Chapter 16

Madeleine said: 'I am two years older than Paul. When we were children, he used to climb into my bed at night for comfort. Later, as we got older, his need for comforting changed. I became aware of the erection that he pressed against my thigh or my buttocks.

'At first, he would just hold it there and I would feel the stiffness throb through his pyjamas. After a while, he would get out of bed and go to the bathroom where he brought himself to a climax.

'Paul has always been very shy. He found it difficult to talk to girls and was so embarrassed if introduced to someone new, that he would stammer. He never had girlfriends. I had boyfriends and had fully discovered sex. I suppose I felt sorry for him.

'When he got into bed with me, he had progressed to leaving off his pyjamas so that he could press himself naked against me. I didn't stop him. Then one night, he came on my thigh instead of going to the bathroom and doing it in private. I pretended I hadn't noticed and from then on he became bolder.

'He was sixteen by then and, like all boys of that age, he had a permanent erection. At first, I pretended to be asleep when he got into bed and would roll on my side to allow him to use my buttocks. He would come on me perhaps four times in a night; I would be swimming in his sperm. His urgency and his hotness turned me on. I would often come myself just by feeling him upon me.

'Sometimes, I really would go to sleep and wake

with him straddling my breasts or with his fingers inside me. He was clumsy and curious and I let him do all these things because I knew he wouldn't get his curiosity or his lust satisfied anywhere else.

'Eventually, I began to guide him and to show him, without speaking, how to use his fingers. I awoke one night and his mouth was between my legs and I wanted to stop him but it felt too good. After I came, he wanted me to use my mouth on him and I felt it was only fair to reciprocate.

'But we never spoke and we never kissed. Kissing was too personal. Kissing was for lovers. Pricks that exploded sperm were biological. A vagina that reacted to external stimuli with an orgasm was physiological We never kissed.'

Bianca resumed touching herself between her legs.

'And did he finally put it inside you?'

'Yes. I had a boyfriend with whom I had sex regularly. It was good sex, strong and fulfilling. One night, I got out of my boyfriend's bed, went home, and got into my own bed. I was still turned on from sex, my vagina was open and wet. Paul climbed in behind me and slipped his erection between my legs and, almost by accident, it went straight inside me.

'After that, he did it every night I would let him and if I was on my period, he would put it in my mouth. It was unspoken sex, secret sex of the night. Much of the time I remained passive, so that I could pretend it wasn't happening, that it was a dream. Eventually, it became a chore. I went away to college to escape what had become nightly duties.'

Bianca said: 'But the photographs were taken recently.'

Madeleine continued: 'Going to college broke the habit. Then Paul went to art school. He was away a year. He didn't make friends because of his shyness. When he left and moved in here, he had the idea of selling erotic pictures to the tourists. But he had no model. I live nearby and I volunteered to pose for him.'

Bianca said: 'And it started again?'

'Not in the same way. This time I controlled it. I could see how aroused he was when he tried to draw me when I was naked or semi-naked. I had lived with my boyfriend for almost two years; my boyfriend was used to seeing my body. But this was a new reaction I was getting from Paul. I enjoyed it, but it meant he couldn't draw very well. He couldn't concentrate.

'I suggested he take photographs and work from them and he got the Polaroid camera. Then I suggested that to make his drawings more erotic, he should be in them, too.'

She smiled.

'It was purely for artistic reasons that I sucked his prick and let him fuck me. From time to time, he says he needs new poses and, if I'm feeling in the mood or my boyfriend is ignoring me, I agree.'

Bianca moaned on her fingers.

Madeleine said: 'Are you jealous?'

'Yes. Exquisitely.' Bianca reached out with her free hand and stroked Madeleine's face. 'I've never done it with a brother.'

She pulled Madeleine's lips towards her own.

Madeleine said: 'Yes, you have. You've done it with my brother.'

They kissed, slow and gentle, and Bianca brought the fingers that had been in her vagina to their mouths and Madeleine licked them.

Madeleine looked into Bianca's eyes and said softly: 'I've never done this before.'

Bianca said: 'When we've finished, you'll want to do it again. And again, and again . . .'

Bianca didn't hear the footsteps on the stairs and

wouldn't have stopped if she had. Her lips were on Madeleine's enlarged clitoris and two fingers of her right hand were moving rhythmically in and out of the young woman's vagina.

If Madeleine had heard the footsteps, she couldn't have stopped.

The door opened and Paul entered, holding a brown paper bag of groceries in his arms. Bianca was vaguely aware of his presence, but continued what she was doing. Madeleine's cries got louder and her breathing got shorter and she came.

As the contractions subsided, Bianca moved around on the bed and slid her sweating body alongside Madeleine's. She kissed the girl's cheek and put an arm around her shoulders to cradle her head. She smiled contentedly at Paul.

'Good,' she said. 'Refreshments.'

Paul put the groceries on the table and stared at the two women, unsure how to react.

Madeleine spoke to him but Bianca didn't understand.

'What did you say?' she asked Madeleine.

'I said we had introduced ourselves.'

Bianca giggled and kissed the girl's shoulder.

'Why not suggest he needs more poses for his drawings?'

Madeleine spoke to him again and he blushed and dropped his head.

Bianca said: 'Paul?'

He raised his head and gave her a sheepish smile. He went to a cupboard and produced a Polaroid camera, a tripod and a cable-release mechanism.

First they sat at the table and drank wine and ate fresh bread. Paul ate his with cheese but the girls smeared theirs with butter and strawberry preserve.

Bianca was now naked and Madeleine wore only ankle socks and Paul stripped off to join the spirit of absurdity for a party without clothes.

Afterwards, the two girls went back to the bed and Paul arranged them into poses and took photographs of them. He was nervous at the start but they saw his nerves dissipate as his penis grew.

He moved them about with hands that became bolder. His guiding touches became caresses. When he moved Madeleine so that a breast hung above Bianca's open mouth, he held the breast in his palm and climbed on the bed behind her and his erection pressed between her legs.

From that moment, he joined the poses and used the cable release as they sweated through an hour of lazy and lascivious enjoyment, during which time he entered both women. They ended the proceedings by sharing him with their mouths.

Afterwards, Bianca stood by the kitchen table looking at the photographs laid out upon its surface. As with the drawings, they showed close-ups of shapes, curves, sexual acts. As with the drawings, they were extremely effective.

Paul lay on the bed, no longer shy, and Bianca talked to Madeleine.

She said: 'Does your brother work for the Doctor?'

Madeleine looked puzzled.

'My brother does not work for a Doctor. He sells his pictures and sometimes he does other things. I know of no Doctor.'

Bianca had begun to suspect that her meeting with Paul had been accidental, a side-effect of her treatment.

'Please ask him if he knows the Doctor?'

Madeleine spoke to him but he shook his head and answered in a negative that even Bianca could understand.

Bianca smiled. She had induced the most satisfying part of her rehabilitation herself.

Madeleine said: 'Who is this Doctor?'

'It doesn't matter. The first time I saw Paul was near the Doctor's consulting rooms. I thought he might know him.'

She smiled at Paul and the young man smiled back.

He said something and Bianca guessed the meaning but Madeleine again translated.

'He says he loves you.'

'Tell him that I love him.' She stroked Madeleine's hair. 'I love you, too.'

They were not idle words; she did love them, with passion and lust and a friendship that was strong because it had not lasted long enough to develop faults.

Paul and Madeleine had helped bring her back to life – they and the Doctor and his machinations.

Tomorrow, he had said, would be a sort of graduation. She looked forward to whatever ceremony he might arrange.

Chapter 17

Graduation had connotations of a first communion so Bianca dressed in a white camisole dress that ended above the knee, white underwear and flat white pumps.

She had applied minimum make-up and looked considerably younger than her thirty years.

When he arrived to collect her from the hotel, Cosmo bowed at her appearance and said: 'My compliments.'

The Doctor smiled when he welcomed her into his consulting room.

He said: 'How very appropriate.'

She lay on the couch and stared at the ceiling that she now knew so well, listened to the Doctor's preliminary small talk and relaxed into the clouds and contours of the land of memories above her.

The Doctor said: 'Yesterday, you talked about arranging your own encounters and sexual adventures.'

'That is correct. Michel encouraged me to do so. His only stipulation was that I tell him about such encounters, in great detail, afterwards.'

'Is there one that particularly stands out in your memory?'

Milan.

'Yes.'

'Can you tell me about it, in the same detail that you afterwards recounted it to your husband?'

'I need to explain the background first.'

'Please do.'

'My husband's company is based in Rome but we have a major branch in Milan that covers northern

Italy. Michel heard that the director in charge of the branch used his power to obtain sexual favours from those he employed. He went there unofficially to investigate and I accompanied him.

'The director was called Lorenzo. He was middle-aged and had the physique of an opera singer, that is, he was overweight although he had once been handsome. In his youth he had had no trouble finding young women with whom to share an affair, although he was married even then. But, like many Italian men, he had the need to continue to prove his virility through seduction.

'Lorenzo was due to appoint a senior manager. It was an important post and one young man was eminently qualified but had hesitated about applying, although Lorenzo had encouraged him to do so. The reason was the young man's wife. She was rumoured to be very attractive. The young man kept her well away from the office and any social functions connected to it, where Lorenzo might meet her. He suspected, with good cause, that the appointment might be dependent upon Lorenzo seducing his wife.

'The situation seemed perfect for exploitation and Michel agreed at once to my proposal. Lorenzo had never met me, and I would pretend to be the young man's wife at a crucial social gathering where the appointment might be discussed and where, we suspected, the young wife's seduction might also be attempted.

'Michel made the arrangements with the young man. He didn't tell him I was his wife, but a woman he had hired specifically for the job. The young man was surprised but agreed. His wife was as lovely as the rumours suggested, but seemed extremely innocent. Perhaps that also had aroused Lorenzo. She was very grateful that I would be taking her place.

'The occasion was a party at Lorenzo's villa. To

stay in character, I wore one of the young woman's outfits. It was a coral-pink evening suit in flimsy material. A small double-breasted jacket that fastened at the waist with one button, a full, soft-pleated skirt. I wore it with her pearls around my neck and with her matching coral-pink underwear. I thought that perhaps, for her husband, she was not so innocent.

'Wine was plentiful at the party and there was a pleasant buffet supper. A trio of musicians played music and, although he was nervous, I felt the young man respond to my body when we danced. He responded more readily than he would have done if he had known who I really was but, of course, he thought my services had been bought and paid for. Lorenzo was delighted we had attended and kissed my hand.

'Later, he called the young man away to talk business. After ten minutes, the young man was back. He said he had been offered the position conditionally: Lorenzo had insisted he interview me also, to ensure I would be an asset to my husband and the company.

'I went to his study, reminding myself that I was supposed to be an innocent young wife, eager to secure her husband's promotion.

'Lorenzo welcomed me into the room and closed the door behind me. I heard the lock click. The room was long, softly lit and thickly carpeted. There was a mahogany desk, a couch, two leather chairs and a small bar. He put a glass of champagne into my hand to toast the promotion of my husband and, in the course of the next few minutes, left me in doubt that for the promotion to be confirmed, I would have to perform a discreet service for him.'

Lorenzo enjoyed the cat-and-mouse game, the power and the anticipation. She could read it all in his eyes and the way he wet his lips with the pink tip of his tongue as he led the conversation from pleasantries to intimacies to proposition.

They were sitting on high stools at the bar.

'Your husband is very fortunate,' he said.

'I realise that, but I can assure you he will repay you for his promotion with the quality of his work.'

'That isn't what I mean. I mean he is very fortunate to have such a beautiful wife.'

Bianca attempted to blush and dropped her gaze.

'You're too kind.'

'Not at all. If I had you as an incentive, there would be nothing I couldn't achieve. Your husband could have had this promotion sooner if he had revealed you before now. You are an asset that should be used.'

'I'm sure I will do all I can to help my husband.'

'That is exactly what I wanted to hear.' He leant forward and rested his hand on her knee above the skirt. 'You must be aware that he has entered a whole new area of career possibilities.'

'He has?'

'Yes indeed. Within a year or two he could move to Rome, or a foreign posting. A seat on the board is not out of the question.'

His hand casually played with the hem of the skirt.

'Really?'

'Oh yes. All things are possible.'

Lorenzo got off the stool, resting his hand on her knee again as if to balance himself, but this time the hand was beneath the material.

Bianca gave a start and closed her legs together protectively.

Lorenzo laughed, as friendly as an uncle.

'There's no need to be nervous, my dear. No need at all.' The hand moved up her leg and she moved her own to stop its progress. 'But I have to make sure that you, too, have the right qualities to go all the way. If you see what I mean?'

'I'll help my husband any way I can.'

'That's what I want to hear.' He pushed his hand

and she gave ground slightly so that his fingers crossed the top of the stocking. He beamed with pleasure. 'Because if the promotion is not confirmed, there is only one alternative.'

'What is that?'

'Demotion.'

'Oh?'

She raised the hand that had been protecting her thigh as if in shock. His hand slid higher still, caressing the flesh at the top of her leg.

'You wouldn't want to ruin his career when he is on the threshold of success, would you, my dear?'

She answered in a low, timorous voice.

'No.'

'Good.'

The fingers dipped over the thigh and stroked the soft inner skin, brushing against her panties.

'Oh please, don't.'

His fingers continued probing.

'But my dear, this is the crucial test of promotion. You have to be willing to make sacrifices for your husband. I have to be sure that you will support him with total dedication.'

'I will,' she whispered.

'Then you will let me continue.'

The fingers dipped beneath the silk panties and found a path through her pubic hair. One finger slid into the mouth of her vagina.

Bianca made herself shake as if in fear.

She said: 'Is there no other way?'

'None.'

She gulped.

'Then what is it that you want of me?'

'Everything.'

The Doctor said: 'Was he specific about the service you were to perform?'

'When he got to the point he intimated he wanted

me to do everything for him sexually.'

'What was your response?'

'I pretended to faint.'

'And?'

'He undressed me.'

Bianca swooned against him and he caught her up in his arms and carried her to the couch. He lay her down and she kept her eyes closed and feigned unconsciousness. She felt him unbutton the jacket and open it. He gasped at the sight and then his fingers unclipped the front fastening of the coral-pink bra and released her breasts.

His hands caressed them and then his mouth was over a nipple. He licked and mauled them and the game she had been playing changed and she felt her own arousal begin.

As he sucked her breasts, he pulled her skirt up to her waist, his hands greedily feeling the curve of her bottom, and pushing between her legs to insert two fingers into her vagina.

She gasped at the intrusion and opened her eyes.

'What are you doing?'

'You know what I'm doing, my dear. I'm going to fuck you.'

He leaned forward to kiss her but she turned away her face.

She said: 'No, not that. That is too intimate.'

He unfastened his trousers, his movements shaky with lust, and knelt on the couch between her legs. He pulled the crutch of the loose panties to one side, positioned his erection and thrust it inside fiercely. It would have hurt if she had not been so wet.

The Doctor said: 'Did he make you do everything?'

'No. He was too anxious, he wanted it too much. He played with my breasts, opened my legs and pushed it inside me. He was rough and he didn't take long.'

'Did you orgasm?'

'No.'

'Did you enjoy the experience?'

'Yes.'

'What happened when he had finished?'

'He resumed his attitude of friendliness. He acted as if what had occurred had been a mutually enjoyable romp. He gave me a vodka martini and made a joke about me enjoying something stiff, then said the promotion would be confirmed in the morning. I would have to report to his office at eleven o'clock to receive the formal notification. He said I should be there alone.'

'And you took that to mean?'

'I took that to mean he would want to resume where he had left off before actually signing the appointment.'

'And did you go to his office the next morning?'

'Yes, I did.'

But before that, she rejoined the young man, and she had an irresistible urge between her legs.

Bianca told him his position was confirmed but suggested they should leave immediately. He was touchingly concerned about what had happened and whether she was alright and she assured him that she was. When they reached the car, he opened the door for her, but she closed it again and pulled him against her.

She kissed him and moved her body against his with no pretence.

'But we shouldn't,' he said.

'Please,' she said, 'I have done you and your wife a service tonight, now you do me a service in return.'

From the strength of his erection, she knew she wouldn't have too much trouble persuading him to comply. She pulled him down a grassy bank away from the parked cars and they lay down. As he hesitated, she unfastened his trousers and persuaded his erection with her mouth.

After that, the young man took charge and he took

Bianca from the front, from behind and with great enthusiasm, and she enjoyed his staying power and his consideration and came four times before he finally finished.

The Doctor said: 'What happened the next day?'

'I went to see Lorenzo at eleven o'clock. I wore a black business suit, with tight skirt and black stockings. I could tell he liked the way I looked. He sat behind the desk in his office and had a document in front of him. I sat in a low chair and he attempted to look up my skirt as we talked.

'He said how much he had enjoyed our meeting the previous evening and how he regretted that we had not had more time together. Perhaps, he said, we could become better friends this morning.

'Then he pushed the document into the middle of the desk and said I had better read it before he signed it. I got up, went to the desk and, because he held the document, I had to lean forward over the side of the desk to read it. As I did so, he got up and walked round the desk until he was behind me. I attempted to straighten up but he kept me in position with one hand in my back. He pulled up my skirt and fucked me.

Bianca knew what was to happen. She felt his hardness against her buttocks when he moved behind her.

'Don't move,' he said.

He slid the tight skirt up to her waist and knelt behind her. His hands felt her white flesh above the black stockings and he licked between her thighs and she felt herself responding. A finger slid between her legs and entered her, then a second and, after a few lubricating movements, Lorenzo used three fingers.

'You're on fire, my dear. An innocent but rampant young woman. You cannot help your desires; enjoy them.'

He stood up, his trousers already open, and guided his prick towards her vagina. She adjusted her position to help him gain entry and he pushed inside with a sigh.

'Is everything to your satisfaction?'

His words were punctuated by his thrusts.

Bianca moved the document.

'You haven't signed it.'

'Plenty of time, my dear. Plenty of time.'

He pushed her forward so that she lay across the desk and he pummelled in and out, holding her steady at the hips. The knock at the door surprised Bianca.

Lorenzo said: 'Come in.'

His secretary opened the door and took one pace inside before she stopped. She was a young and attractive woman and Bianca wondered whether she, too, had been treated this way. They exchanged looks but Lorenzo did not break his rhythm.

The woman said: 'The gentleman you were expecting is here.'

'Good. Send him in.'

The young woman left the room briefly, and returned to escort the gentleman Lorenzo had been expecting. It was Michel. She showed him into the office and left for good, closing the door.

Lorenzo still didn't change his position or slow his rhythm. Instead, he reached across Bianca's back to shake hands with her husband.

'This is the young lady I was telling you about. Beautiful, isn't she? She'll do anything for the company.'

Michel looked into Bianca's face.

'Anything?'

'Anything. Won't you my dear?'

He withdrew and helped her stand up but the skirt was so tight it remained around her waist. She could feel his prick resting against her bottom.

Lorenzo reached round her front and unfastened

the buttons of the jacket and opened it. She wore nothing beneath it.

Michel said: 'Beautiful indeed.' He touched her breasts. 'Anything?'

'Anything. Isn't that right, my dear?' Lorenzo pressed himself close against her back, talking softly in her ear. 'This is the owner of the company. I'm sure you want to display your loyalty to him, don't you?'

Bianca licked her lips as she stared at Michel.

'Yes.'

'Good girl.' To Michel, he said: 'What would your pleasure be?'

Michel unfastened his trousers and sat on the leather couch.

'It seems a shame to let that mouth go to waste,' he said.

'It does indeed. On your hands and knees, my dear. Show your loyalty.'

He pushed Bianca forward and she knelt before her husband, caressed his familiar penis, blew him a kiss and bent forward to take it in her mouth. Behind her, Lorenzo knelt and re-entered her vagina.

Michel caressed her hair absently whilst Lorenzo thrust energetically, as if anxious to prove his virility to his boss as well as the wives of his junior executives.

Her husband said: 'We should not take too long over this. There is work to be done.'

'Of course, sir.'

Lorenzo speeded up and she squirmed against him, openly for the first time, and timed the movements of her fingers at the base of Michel's prick and of the ministerings of her mouth. The slight pressure of a finger on her cheek made her look up and he motioned for her to slow down.

The director of the Milan branch finished, containing his grunts and groans because of the superior company he was keeping. Michel remained seated with Bianca's head in his lap.

Michel said: 'Perhaps you would leave us for a few minutes? There are other things I would wish to do in private.'

'Of course, sir.'

She heard Lorenzo get up and fasten his clothes and leave the office. Michel raised her head and brought her up to sit next to him on the couch.

'Enjoying yourself? he said.

She licked her lips, still wet with his juices.

'Immensely.'

They kissed and slid from the couch to the floor and made love and she came, loudly, loud enough for Lorenzo and his secretary to hear outside, and she came again, louder still.

The Doctor said: 'Did the young man get his promotion?'

'Oh yes.'

'And what happened to Lorenzo?'

'He was fired.'

'Did you feel any guilt about leading Lorenzo into a trap?'

'I felt no guilt. It was Lorenzo's own trap. He enjoyed setting it and he enjoyed using his power to make me succumb to his demands. He wouldn't have enjoyed it half so much if he had known how much I enjoyed it. Lorenzo was close to a rapist. He deserved to lose his job. He deserved to be caught in his own trap.'

'Have you ever set a trap?'

'Of course. I trapped my uncle as soon as I climbed into his bed. I attempted to trap Michel by climbing a tree. Seduction can often be a set of traps but they are acceptable as long as intimidation or coercion are not used.'

'Is deceit acceptable?'

Bianca considered the question.

'Role-playing and temptation, I think, are acceptable. Pretending, is acceptable.'

'You equivocate, Bianca. Have you ever used deceit?'

'I suppose what I did in the hotel room in Zurich was deceitful, but not in a harmful way. The young boy could have left the room without touching me but he chose not to.'

'Perhaps your deceit left the young boy feeling guilty. Did you think of that?'

'No. He might have worried in case he was found out but he would not have felt guilt. No young man would; most young men would have been extremely grateful for the opportunity.' She smiled. 'Besides, Michel put the young boy's mind at rest when we left the hotel the next day. He tipped him handsomely and told him I had been fully satisfied by his services.'

'But isn't that playing with people's emotions, with their lives?'

'If it is, it's a very pleasant game and I have had no complaints.'

'None?'

She hesitated.

'Perhaps . . .'

'Go on, Bianca.'

'There was one occasion when we used deceit. But it was for a very good reason.'

'And that was?'

'To test friendship.'

'Tell me about it.'

Chapter 18

A day in the country, with wine, the warmth of summer, the smell of the earth, and the pervading possibility of stolen sex.

Bianca said: 'It involved two men who sought Michel out after we had been married for three or four years. They had all gone to the same school. They wanted his financial backing for a business proposition and, in the course of their talks, they made great efforts to rekindle the friendship they had shared years before.

'Michel, however, confided to me that he didn't remember the former friendship being as deep and warm as they said it was. I suggested that we test its veracity.'

'How?'

'By leading them into temptation and seeing if they would seduce the wife of the man they called friend.'

'Go on.'

'Their names were Carl and Georges. Carl was the same height as my husband but thinner. He was sharp-featured and rather timid; always polite, a man in a suit who would willingly demur in conversation rather than risk causing offence. Georges was bigger, a strong man who was blunt in conversation but never unpleasant. Carl seemed to have no character; Georges seemed to be confining his until they got the backing for their deal. They were both sycophantic in their friendship to Michel and, in consequence, in the way they behaved towards me.

'Michel invited them to be our guests at our country house. On the last day of their stay, we suggested a picnic. Our estates were large and we drove a mile from the house, taking a narrow track through the woods. We left the car and walked a hundred yards to a clearing on a river bank that Michel and I knew well. The grass was soft, the place secluded.

'We ate lobster and oysters and drank champagne. There was fresh bread and cheese and fruit and, after the champagne, a case of mixed wines, some of which we cooled in the river, and a bottle of Marsala, the fortified Italian wine. We had already established that Carl and Georges didn't like it and the bottle was for me. Its alcoholic content had, of course, been much diluted so that I wouldn't get drunk.

'The conversation was relaxed and Michel talked of friendship and trust. Carl and Georges agreed they had all been lucky at bonding so early at school – a bonding, they said, that would never be broken by deceit or dishonour.

'I wore a simple summer dress in pink and lilac that buttoned down the front. The dress was open to my thighs and I went barefoot to feel the grass in my toes and for when I paddled in the river. If I stood in a certain position on the bank, I knew the sun turned the material of the dress diaphanous and that my companions could see my body. I also noticed that Carl and Georges, not unnaturally, took every opportunity to look if they believed themselves to be unobserved.

'After two hours and several bottles of wine, Michel received a call on his portable telephone that summoned him back to the house. He made his apologies at having to abandon us and left the telephone with us. He said he would be unable to return but that we should use the telephone when we wanted a chauffeur to collect us.

'I was lying next to Michel and he kissed me before he got up to leave. It was a deep kiss and I responded to it with my body, as if the wine had had an effect on my emotions. I pushed my hips against his thigh and wound my leg around him. He laughed when we broke apart and said, loud enough for the two men to hear, "Later".

'Before he went, he told Carl and Georges that I was now in their care and he asked them, out of earshot of me, not to let me drink too much Marsala as the strength could put me in a stupor.

'He went and, a few moments later, Carl disappeared into the woods after him. Georges sat with his back against a tree and I rested my head upon his thigh. He poured me a glass of Marsala and I drank it. Carl returned and I heard him whisper that Michel had, indeed, driven back to the house. Georges offered me more Marsala and, a few glasses later, I told him the sun and the drink had made me sleepy.

'Georges said I should have a nap and he changed positions to make me more comfortable. He lay me between his legs so that my face lay on his thigh and I pretended to drift into sleep, moving again to find comfort. His hands moved me gently and my head was turned so that it lay in his lap. I could feel his erection against my cheek through his trousers; I could smell his desire.

'I snuggled my head against him and his erection throbbed and he rubbed it against me, not in an obvious manner, but as if he, too, was getting comfortable. I didn't object; I continued to doze.'

Carl was by her feet, looking up her skirt.

He said: 'What do you think?' His voice was tight and urgent.

Georges said: 'I think I may come in my trousers.'

He moved his erection more firmly against Bianca's face.

She felt the skirt of the dress being parted. Another button was unfastened and it was parted more, then another button so that the white panties that she wore were revealed.

Carl said: 'Oh my God.'

Georges moved gently but rhythmically against her face. His hand slipped over the front of the dress and he felt the outline of her breasts with careful fingers.

Carl said: 'Wake her.'

'I don't want to wake her. I want to fuck her.'

'Wake her first. See if you can wake her. If you do, give her some more wine. If she remains unconscious . . .'

He left the proposition unfinished.

Georges shook her shoulders.

'Bianca? Wake up, Bianca.'

Bianca moved sleepily.

'Michel?' She said. She moved her face deliberately against the outline of the erection. 'Mmm, Michel.'

Georges said: 'Yes, it's Michel.'

This time his hand went inside the dress and caressed her breasts. She moaned at the touch. After a while, he unfastened his trousers and moved her head. His penis was now released and hot against her face. He moved it against her neck and over her cheek. When it reached her lips, she parted them and allowed it to slip inside.

Georges said: 'Oh God. Oh God.'

'Michel,' Bianca mumbled, as she sucked.

'Yes,' he whispered. 'Michel.'

At her feet, she heard Carl unfasten his trousers and begin to masturbate as he watched.

As if in a daze, she moved sufficiently to release her right hand from beneath her body and she used her fingers around the base of the prick that was in her mouth. Her fingernails scratched at his testicles whilst she gripped the base between thumb and forefinger. It was not long before he came, attempting to control the vigour of his discharge for fear of disturbing her sleepiness. She swallowed it all down, in long gulps. It tasted like the oysters she had swallowed earlier.

Georges disengaged himself and she was lying on her back on the grass. Someone began to tug at her panties.

'No, you can't,' said Georges.

'You've had your turn, now it's mine.'

'But she might wake up.'

'She won't wake up.'

Carl's voice was taut as wire.

Bianca allowed her buttocks to be raised and her panties to be removed. Her legs were parted and fingers opened the lips of her vagina. A sharp tongue dipped into the hotness. Carl slurped greedily, a delicious noise that made Bianca move her hips. His sharp nose dipped also, and rubbed her clitoris, and made her moan out loud.

He paused and raised his head.

'You see. The bitch is loving it. She doesn't know and doesn't care who's fucking her. She just wants to be fucked.'

Bianca said: 'Michel . . .?'

Georges leaned close and replied.

'Yes,' he said. 'It's Michel.'

Carl's face was between her legs again. He licked her from the start of her vaginal valley, over her clitoris, around the lips and into the canyon of her opening, and along the narrow channel to her tight anus.

She raised her knees, her feet flat on the ground, and responded with her hips.

Carl knelt between her thighs and pushed the head of his erection into the hot mouth of her sex. He pushed, an inch at a time, and she gasped as she discovered how big it was, in circumference and length.

He filled her, holding it deep, before he started his

thrusts and she could tell by his disjointed movements that he was too excited to last.

Georges was of the same opinion.

'Not inside her,' he said anxiously. 'She may notice.'

But Carl could not stop, could not withdraw if he had wanted to. He began yelling before his orgasm started and kept on yelling as he emptied himself inside her.

The Doctor said: 'What did they do, Bianca?'

'Georges came in my mouth and Carl fucked me, although Georges told him not to. Afterwards they argued because he had shed his sperm where I might feel it and suspect. But they became reassured when I still didn't wake up and Carl said that when they had finished, they could put me in the river so that the water would wash away the sperm. They could say I fell in after drinking too much and that they saved me.

'And is that what they did?'

'Yes. They both had me again, changing my position and becoming bolder when my eyes remained closed. Georges was gentle but Carl was harsh. After he had used my mouth and taken me from behind he wanted to sodomise me but Georges wouldn't let him. He said that no matter how drunk I was, I would certainly notice the condition of my anus if he sodomised me with a weapon of that size. I would have, too.'

'So how did it end?'

'They both came again, inside me. Then they had a drink and smoked cigars and let me sleep some more, to allow the swelling of my vagina to subside. Eventually, when I began to stir, they carried me to the river and lowered me into the water.

'At this, I ended my pretended stupor and they helped me back onto the bank. They said I had gone into the bushes to relieve myself and must have fallen in. They apologised at not realising how intoxicated I had been and handed me back my panties. I accepted them with a blush.

'They telephoned for the chauffeur and they wrapped me in a blanket and were most solicitous about my condition.'

The Doctor said: 'What was the outcome?'

'That night, after dinner, we showed them the video Michel had made of the whole proceedings.'

'A video?'

'Yes. Michel had hidden three cameras around the clearing and they had recorded everything that had occurred. He had enjoyed editing the results into what was a rather erotic hour-long film.'

'And?'

'And Georges pretended to be overcome with remorse and asked for forgiveness in the name of their friendship, which Michel denied. Carl knew what the outcome would be immediately and left the room to pack. They both left early the next morning, minus a friendship and minus the financial backing they had wanted.'

'But was that fair, Bianca? Wouldn't the situation have tempted the closest friend?'

'Of course any friend would have been tempted. But if the friend were honourable – and friendship should be honourable – he wouldn't have encouraged my stupor by plying me with strong drink. If I had fallen into a stupor of my own accord, an honourable friend wouldn't have taken his sexual pleasure whilst I lay unconscious.'

The Doctor said: 'Did Carl and Georges give you an orgasm?'

'Oh yes. I came three times.'

'Was it apparent that you orgasmed?'

'Oh yes.'

'Couldn't that be construed as encouragement?'

'No. They provided me with orgasms under false

pretence. They were pretending to be my husband.'

The Doctor paused.

'Did you like what happened?'

'Very much so. I liked having no control at their hands and yet having total control over their future. I also liked watching the video afterwards with Michel.'

The Doctor got to his feet. He smiled at Bianca.

'I think we have explored your past enough, Bianca. I have enjoyed listening to you, and I hope you have enjoyed remembering.'

'I have.'

'Then I shall leave you for a few moments while I make sure that other arrangements are in hand. Leave the couch at your leisure and leave behind the past, for the couch is where you confronted and recalled the past. When I return, we shall talk briefly about the future.'

He left the room and Bianca stared at the ceiling that was like a bank of white clouds through which she had flown on her memories. She had found the sessions pleasurable, she had become aroused by the incidents of the past and she was reluctant to leave them.

But, of course, she wouldn't be leaving them. They would always be with her, and she also had Michel's videos of their times and adventures together.

She left the couch and sat in an armchair and waited patiently.

The Doctor returned and sat in an armchair opposite.

'We have almost come to the conclusion of our conversations,' he said.

'I'm sorry,' she said. 'I have enjoyed them.'

He nodded and smiled.

'Tell me, Bianca. Is there any sexual episode that you regret?'

'None.'

'Even long ago when that first boyfriend abused you?'

'No, even that had its good points. I was not harmed and it was part of a learning process. It also provided me with moments I could recall when I was alone and which I could turn into orgasms. It helped me begin to understand sex.'

The Doctor said: 'Do you understand sex?'

'Sex is very simple. It is a physical act that provides the ultimate enjoyment. But mankind has been burdened with guilt about its practice ever since man created gods and began living to their rules.

'Man created God and society and, to protect its ordered continuity, declared that sex was only to be practised within marriage in the name of love.

'In society's eyes, sex was only respectable in the context of love and marriage. That is because society is frightened that the secret might escape and spoil its rules and regulations.

'Love does add an extra dimension but it is not essential for the enjoyment of sex. Pure sex is liberating and fulfilling. But most individuals cannot enjoy sex for its own purity because they clothe it with their own fears, prejudices, prides and jealousies. Society has robbed them of the ability to embrace it with their emotions naked.'

The Doctor said: 'And what is the secret of sex, Bianca?'

'The secret is very simple. It is: enjoy.'

The Doctor smiled and nodded.

He said: 'Excellent, Bianca. Excellent. You have rediscovered yourself. The frankness of your memories and every deed practiced upon your body has helped to free your soul.

'The psychologist Maslow found that women are divided into three groups: of high, medium and low dominance. The high-dominance woman is highly sexed, enjoys sex in all its varieties, and harbours no guilt about its practice.

'The high-dominance woman also needs a high-dominance man; a man to respect, a man who will respect her. You had that with Michel. It was always going to be hard to replace him and the combination of love, memories and respect, made it more difficult.

'Sartre said that emotion is a substitute for action. A man and woman in love release their desire in sex. But if one of them rejects the other, the desire continues to grow within the reject's heart. It becomes wild and passionate. The rejected one becomes entirely possessed by an emotion that is a substitute for sex.

'That is what happened when you lost Michel. You saw his death as a rejection and your desires grew out of control, yet you repressed them in his memory. Your tensions needed to be released. Your desire needed to be fulfilled. That is what we have achieved. Congratulations, Bianca. You are now ready for your baptism into your new life.'

Chapter 19

The Doctor led her to the room where she had met the Blind Man. Before he opened the door, he took a mask from a chair in the hall and handed it to Bianca.

'Please put it on.'

It was a blindfold: soft pads for her eyes that were held in place around her head by an elasticated band. She could see nothing. She was as blind as the Blind Man.

The Doctor said: 'My guests are here for your pleasure. Enjoy.'

He led her forward and she heard the door open. In the room, people who had been chatting as if at a cocktail party, became suddenly silent.

The Doctor led her forward by the arm and she heard the door close. She sensed the people around her but had no idea how many there were.

'Ladies and gentlemen,' the Doctor said, 'I present Bianca.'

She felt a tremor of panic when he let go of her arm, but the gathering began to applaud, a polite but friendly burst of clapping. Someone lifted her right hand and placed in it a fluted glass.

'Champagne, my dear', a man said. 'The toast is to you.'

'Bianca!'

Her name was echoed by eight, nine, twelve people . . . she really had no idea. She drank the champagne and someone took the empty glass from her hand and replaced it with a full one. She drank that, too, but refused a third when it was offered.

Music began to play. Gentle American soul music, a black voice and the rhythm softened by a string section.

'Bianca,' a man said. 'Grant me this dance?'

'Of course.'

He took her in his arms and they danced slowly. He moved close and she didn't object. She could feel his penis stirring in his trousers. As they swayed, she moved her hips against it and made it stiffen.

'Bianca, Bianca,' the man whispered, kissing her neck. 'Keep moving like that and you'll make me come.'

People talked discreetly around her. They were obviously watching as she slowly ground her hips against the now rampant prick that pressed against her.

The man licked her neck and she listened to the increasing raggedness of his breath. His arms were hooked beneath her arms and his hands held her shoulders.

'Oh yes, oh please, Bianca. Make me come. Make me come.'

The words were whispered into her ear, his tongue flicking at the lobe, his breath gasping, and she held his hips and pulled him closer, opening her thighs and raising herself on her toes to rub the length of her vagina down his erection.

'Bianca . . .'

Her name was a sigh as he came, holding himself against her, pulsing his sperm into his trousers.

There was a ripple of approval from the onlookers and as her partner sagged, she was guided away by other hands. A fresh erection was against her buttocks, the man's hands upon her breasts.

She moved herself back against it and heard him gasp and they were joined by a second man who pressed himself hard against her front.

The pressure of their bodies held her up and she allowed herself to float on a wave of sexuality as they moved slowly and deliberately to the music and the rhythm of their groins.

Their mouths licked her neck, kissed her face; their hands explored her body over her dress, caressing curves, squeezing flesh.

And all the time, their erections pushed against her and she moved her hips backwards and forwards, grinding against the one between her buttocks on the backward thrust and against the one that was at her vagina on the forward thrust.

Conversation around them had stopped and she was aware of the gasps and sighs of the onlookers as the two men slowly raised her dress. It slid upwards, across the nylon of the stockings and the silk of her flesh, until it was round her waist.

Hands also opened her bodice to free her breasts and the two men pressed ever harder against her, taking grips on her breasts and her hips.

Bianca's body was exposed but their own bodies were still fully clothed, as they came, almost together. She cried out at the feeling of their pricks pulsing and jumping.

Someone led her, senses reeling, to a low couch or chaise longue. She was encouraged to sit at the end and lay back so that her feet were on the floor whilst her head rested on a cushion.

Her dress was raised again and her legs parted; fingernails scratched patterns on her stockinged thighs and lips kissed their way along the nylon upwards from her knee, crossed onto skin and licked onwards, following the path made by a strap of her garter belt.

As the strap crossed her groin, the lips left it and licked along the crease of her flesh, going down, beneath the loose leg of her panties, to nibble at her pubic hair, the fingers searching their way ahead towards the glistening dampness between her legs.

Bianca did not know whether the fingers and the mouth belonged to a man or woman and she did not care. She gasped loudly and moved her hips to encourage their progress and moaned when a finger finally opened the groove of her vagina. The lips followed and enclosed it, mouth to mouth, a tongue dug deeply inside her and a moist finger, lubricated from its vaginal delving, traced further between her legs and probed her anus.

She clamped the head of her unknown lover between her thighs and moved her hips, attempting to fuck the mouth, but other hands gripped her legs and parted them again and the mouth was removed.

People were on all sides, hands were touching her body all over, exploring every crevice and every soft place. Mouths sucked at her nipples, her arms were stretched above her and tongues licked the sweat from her armpits, hands stroked her thighs.

A finger was inside her anus and a man was rubbing his erection against the ankle of her left leg, while a woman had straddled her right leg and was bringing herself off against her knee.

Another woman pushed one of Bianca's hands beneath her skirt and inserted her fingers into herself, and a man held the palm of her other hand against the front of his trousers and rubbed himself against it.

All around her, the party guests came while she rolled on the couch, her mouth open – hoping, expecting, begging for another mouth to kiss, a prick to suck, a vagina to lick, but none were offered.

The itch between her legs was unbearable and all the ministrations to her were designed to build her sexual tensions but avoid an orgasm.

She rode on the edge of ecstasy, the noises from her throat no longer human, her skin being charged from every touch, every probe, every grunt from someone else's coming but not being allowed to climb that final peak herself.

Finally, the hands, the bodies and the mouths left her. She lay alone on the couch and, as her wits returned, her right hand moved down her body towards the point where all her senses were concentrated.

'No, Bianca.'

It was the Doctor's voice.

'But I need . . .'

'Yes, Bianca. You need sex. That was the purpose of your visits here. Now it is time to leave the safety of a controlled experiment and find it for yourself. Your graduation is complete.'

A hand took hers and indicated that she should get to her feet. She did so, and took a few moments to gain her balance, her body trembling from what it had undergone and still aching for relief.

The Doctor led her back across the room and, as she left, the clapping started again, the people who had enjoyed her so aesthetically without spilling any seed upon her, marking her graduation with applause that lasted until the door opened and closed, leaving the people inside the room, still unseen, and Bianca outside in the hall, still blindfolded.

'You no longer need this,' the Doctor said, and removed the pads from her eyes.

Bianca almost regretted being able to see again. The experience of having one of her senses removed had heightened all the others and the intrusion of sight immediately lessened the intensity of the recent memory of what she had just enjoyed.

She was aware that her bodice gaped and fastened just enough of the buttons to almost make it decent. The Doctor held out her shoulder bag and escorted her through the hall.

He opened the door and shook her hand.

A soft summer breeze flirted with her skirt.

Bianca said: 'Thank you, for all you have done.'

The Doctor smiled and said: 'Now you are on your own. Go and find your own excitement. And enjoy.'

Bianca returned his smile, and raised her hand to flick hair that the breeze had blown across her face, and caught the aroma on the fingers that had helped an unknown woman to orgasm.

She held them to her nose and the memory of what had just occurred filled her senses.

'I will,' she said, and crossed the courtyard to the street without looking back, determined that her graduation would not be complete until she had fulfilled her daily ritual with the young man . . . and added one final ceremony.

Chapter 20

Paul and Madeleine were in the café by the Metro station where she had arranged to meet them.

The day before, she hadn't known how she would feel after her final session with the Doctor, but she had sensed that she would not wish to lose momentum by returning to the young man's apartment. Safe sex in his apartment was now in the past, another pleasant memory for which she would always be grateful.

Bianca did not know whether or not she would see the brother and sister again after today.

Perhaps in a few weeks or a few months she might get lonely for their simple and undemanding companionship and their unique relationship, and invite them to Italy or the villa by the Mediterranean for a holiday. Perhaps she wouldn't.

Life was exciting again and there were other people to meet in other parts of the world, other adventures upon which to embark, the possibility of meeting another man with whom she could share adventures and life as fully as she had with Michel.

Everything was possible again and she wanted no restrictions upon the possibilities.

Paul rose from his seat when she approached and Madeleine smiled. Bianca, still aroused from the Doctor's ceremony, saw them as the vibrant young couple with whom she had copulated the day before and with whom she wanted to copulate again. Now.

They saw the wildness in her eyes, the flush in her face and caught the tension from her.

No words needed to be spoken, indeed, Bianca couldn't speak for the desire in her throat. She licked her lips and looked from the sister to the brother.

Madeleine dropped some money on the table and they left the café.

None of them knew exactly where they were going until Bianca saw the dress shop where she had first seen Paul and Madeleine. She pointed at the shop, they crossed the road and went inside.

There were few other customers browsing amongst the racks of dresses and the assistants preferred to sit by the sales tills.

Bianca took two dresses from a rack and they went to the changing rooms at the back of the shop. She pulled Madeleine into the end cubicle, pulled the curtain and dropped the dresses on the floor.

They went into each other's arms, their mouths greedy for each other. Their tongues fought like snakes and they exchanged saliva. Madeleine was ready for an illicit encounter but was taken aback by Bianca's passion.

She found herself forced back against the wall as the woman who had introduced her to the delights of female sex, moved her body against hers, ran her hands over her, mauled her breasts and raised her skirt.

The French girl was breathless, her pulse racing, as Bianca's hands went into her panties and her fingers dipped into her sex. Two fingers slipped inside without preliminaries and began to move rhythmically in and out. They made a delicious slurping noise and released a smell of sex that filled the small cubicle.

Madeleine gave herself up to the pleasure, her eyes half closed, but when Bianca's thumb brushed against her clitoris she could not help but moan out loud. Bianca covered her mouth with her own and swallowed the moans as she kept up the rhythm.

Neither of them were fully aware of their surroundings or the noises they were making in the confines of the changing room. All perceptions of the normal world beyond the curtain were lost in a haze of marvellously desperate longing.

Bianca dropped to her knees and pulled Madeleine's white panties far enough down her thighs to give her access to her vagina.

Now her mouth covered that pleasure mouth and was greedy all over again in a new and sensuous way. Her tongue dug deep for the juices inside the young woman, before licking along the groove to capture her clitoris between her lips. Her hands caressed her buttocks.

There was nothing to stop Madeleine's moans now and they came rhythmically, in time to Bianca's sucking and licking.

Outside the cubicle, Bianca was only vaguely aware of raised voices in argument. She didn't care what was happening outside the cubicle. All that mattered was here, in this small space; all that mattered was here, at the conjunction of these girlish thighs, this beautifully aromatic bushy swampland that she ploughed with her tongue and mouth and face.

Madeleine's moans stopped, she held her breath for an achingly tense moment, and then came. Her body shuddered around the epicentre of its quake, her voice was loud: a wail of anguish, release and joy.

Bianca was aware that the curtain was no longer closed. She kissed Madeleine's vagina gently and turned her head. A woman, who wore a name tag on her dress, stared down at her. Her expression was dominated by shock and her lips worked soundlessly as if searching for words of distaste, but Bianca also saw something else in her eyes: fascination, perhaps, or desire.

Maybe the shock was because the woman was

experiencing feelings that she had never before acknowledged; perhaps she was envious of Madeleine's state of wonderful exhaustion.

Paul was looking nervously towards the rest of the shop and speaking rapidly to the woman in a low voice, although what excuses he could possibly be making, Bianca could not imagine.

She got to her feet and smiled hazily at the woman, aware that her face bore traces of Madeleine's juices. Alongside her, Madeleine recovered, straightened her clothing, and took a deep breath.

Bianca said to the woman: 'I am sorry you have been disturbed.'

She said the words with deliberate irony and motioned with her head that Madeleine should translate. The girl did.

The woman came out of her trance. She gulped, licked her lips and avoided Bianca's gaze. Instead, she picked up the dresses that were on the floor.

Bianca and Madeleine moved slowly past her out of the cubicle. At the steps at the end of the changing area, four young women stared at them, eyes wide in disbelief.

'You must have made a lot of noise,' Bianca said to Madeleine.

They laughed, held hands and walked from the shop with Paul behind them.

There was still Paul. Bianca had to salve her conscience and establish her re-birth with Paul as well, but where to take him?

Madeleine sensed what Bianca was looking for and they left the shopping street and took a narrow avenue that ended at a tall wall. Halfway down was an alley between the properties. Its cobbles were littered with rubbish and there was an industrial wastebin by the back door of a Cantonese restaurant.

They ran down the alley and past the bin.

The location was dirty, disreputable and almost public. At the end of the alley were the iron railings of a small park.

Bianca thought it was perfect.

She pulled Paul against the wall and kissed him open-mouthed. He hesitated at the suddenness of the onslaught but quickly responded when her urgency once again transferred itself to his body.

He pulled her dress to her waist and his hands were demanding as they moved over her buttocks and between her legs, finding her wet and hot.

Bianca grappled with his Levis, pulling them apart at the front and pulling his erection free from his underpants. With the excitement they were generating, she knew it would not take him long once he was inside her.

She crouched before him and put the head of his prick in her mouth. Above her, he leaned against the wall with both hands and groaned as she used her mouth and her fingers. She released his cock from her mouth to rub it against her face and, in doing so, looked towards at the iron railings of the park.

Beyond the railings, locked inside the park and locked inside yet another world, was an elderly man. He wore shapeless trousers that were held up by braces, a shirt whose sleeves were rolled back, and a beret. He smoked a pipe and he watched them intently.

The thrill of an audience, even so small an audience, ran through Bianca and she took Paul's erection back into her mouth and fellated him again, ensuring that the elderly man could see all that she did. When Paul began to withdraw because the pleasure was getting too great, she released him again and stood upright.

They kissed again and, Madeleine being alongside them, they kissed Madeleine as well, all three now aware of the man who watched from beyond the railings.

Bianca turned to face the wall and leaned forward to rest her arms against it. She turned her head to watch the elderly spectator. Paul raised the dress again, manoeuvred the panties to one side, and entered her from behind.

She cried out at their combined heat and he held himself steady inside her as he attempted to control the intensity of feelings. A small cry was warning that he was unable to do so, and he gave three, four, five great thrusts and he orgasmed, releasing sperm and a yell that echoed between the high walls of the alley.

Bianca enjoyed the thrill of his release and the thrill of being watched by the man in the beret but she again held back her own orgasm.

Paul slipped from her and she stood upright. The dress fell back into position and she allowed her breathing to return to normal. She stared at the elderly man, who puffed steadily on his pipe.

Madeleine and Paul were ready to go and she allowed them to move a few paces ahead before she looked again at the elderly man, whose stance had not changed from beginning to end of the encounter, and who could have been painted by Matisse.

She blew him a kiss on her fingers.

He took the pipe from his mouth, smiled, and caught the kiss with puckered lips.

Chapter 21

They parted without promises, still friends and lovers. Madeleine led Paul away and Bianca watched them until they turned a corner and disappeared from sight.

Her own graduation ceremony still lay ahead, one she would undertake in remembrance of Michel and, in a way, to shed the influence of Michel. One she would organise herself.

She walked slowly through the streets, her body tingling with the day's sexual progress that had started at the hotel, when she had chosen the clothes she would wear for this special day.

The excitement had built up ever since, through the memories she had recalled on the Doctor's couch, through the hands and enclosed pricks of the guests at the Doctor's cocktail party, and through the way she had elicited public orgasms from Madeleine and Paul.

During this time, she had held herself in check, been denied release when she had expected and wanted it, and held herself in check again. Now it was her turn to find release and she walked sensuously along the pavement, aware of the looks that every man who passed gave her, aware of her breasts almost hanging free inside her open bodice, aware of the perfume of sex that pervaded her every pore.

She retraced the steps she had taken the first time she had followed Paul from the metro station, when he had been simply the anonymous 'young man' and she had been walking into the unknown.

Now she was walking into a different kind of unknown, filled with possibilities that made her vagina twitch in anticipation and released butterflies of desire and trepidation in the pit of her stomach.

She found the sidestreet and the derelict house. The noises of distant traffic and nearer demolition were the same, the heat and the dust were the same. The boarded doorway was the same.

Bianca entered and climbed the stairs. She went into the room that had no outer wall and walked carefully to the edge of the floorboards.

On the demolition and construction site beyond, a crane from which a lead weight hung, stood idle. Two men swung picks and a third shook with the vibrations of a powerdrill. The men all worked stripped to the waist, their bodies rippling with muscle, sweat and dirt.

Bianca moistened her lips with her tongue. She could taste her desire.

She looked at her watch. It was almost the same time as when the young man had left her here after taking her swiftly and silently from behind. She remembered the moment, the aftermath of silence as the work outside had stopped and she had heard the men approaching; she remembered her fear.

The man holding the powerdrill looked up slowly, as if alerted by the strength of her gaze. His eyes locked with hers and then she saw them move onto her body, and felt them as they unashamedly undressed and raped her.

He switched off the drill and said something to his companions. They, too, stopped work and looked up at her, as she stood, open-legged at the edge of the room with no wall, the breeze lifting the skirt of her dress, the bodice hanging open with promise.

The man lay the powerdrill down on its side and the others dropped the picks. They began to walk towards the house, slowly, without hurry, as if they sensed she would not run away, that she had come just for them.

Bianca went into the other room, the room that had the kitchen table and the empty window through which spilled a halo of light from the mouth of God. She unfastened the buttons of the dress and removed it, folding it carefully so that it would be clean when it was all over, and laying it in a corner on top of her bag.

The men's footsteps were on the stairs, coming closer, too close now to run, but then she had never contemplated running. She walked into the middle of the room, every inch of her body alive with excitement.

A trickle of sweat curved down her breast and she watched its progress. Her breasts were full, the nipples erect. The muscles of her vagina were contracting in spasm.

She again licked her lips and called out: 'In here.'

They followed the sound of her voice and stopped at the open door, staring in disbelief at what they saw: Bianca, naked but for white garter belt and panties, stockings and shoes.

Her eyes were glazed and she saw them only as three men rather than individuals. The one who had used the drill was a giant, another had long blond hair, and the third had a cropped head that made him look evil and tattoos along both his arms from hands to shoulders.

The men stepped slowly into the room, the giant directly in front of her, the blond to her left and the evil one to her right.

Now it was their turn to lick their lips as their eyes moved lewdly over her body. The evil one began to speak but the giant silenced him with one word, as if he believed that speech might break the spell and Bianca might start screaming.

She opened her mouth and her tongue flicked over her teeth; her eyes flashed in anticipation and they knew she would not scream, at least not for help.

The giant stepped forward, reached out a huge hand and stroked her face. She turned her head against it and took his thumb into her mouth, sucking the dirt from it and biting it gently in her teeth.

He grunted in lust as he realised how ready she was and pulled her close with his other arm, crushing her against his body, his mouth over hers, his tongue bruising its way past her lips.

Bianca sucked on his tongue and ran her nails down the muscles of his back whilst grinding her hips against the rough cloth of his trousers. His right hand reached down and ripped the panties, the material cutting into her as it shredded and making her cry out, half in pain, half in ecstasy.

He said something to his companions and they moved for the first time, lifting her and lying her on her back on the table. The giant unfastened and pushed down his trousers but, from her position, Bianca could not see the size of his penis.

The giant lifted her legs and pushed a finger, then two fingers, inside her vagina, and she yelled out. He withdrew the fingers and she arched herself to prepare for his real onslaught and he began to feed his prick inside her, inch after inch, until she thought it would never end.

She gasped as he pressed ever deeper until she had accepted it all and stared up into his face with eyes that were wide and staring, unaware of the hands of the other two that groped her breasts. He withdrew and thrust and she yelled loudly and continued to yell in time to his powerful movements.

Her legs were draped over the giant's arms and he reached forward and knocked the other two men aside to grab her breasts for himself.

If she had not been so wet and so well-prepared, even she might not have managed to take him at the first attempt, but because she was so ready, she had not just taken him, she had welcomed him, and now she delighted in his power and the throb of a prick that seemed to fill her up to her waist.

Her hips pounded back against his and they yelled into each other's faces as she felt the orgasm begin to build. The pressure and the pleasure increased and her yell changed into one long continuous rising moan.

The giant responded with fiercer, more desperate thrusts, but she did not wait for him. She welcomed her own tidal wave of pleasure and let it overwhelm her in a total release that went on forever. As it began to ebb, the giant came and the deep pulse of his prick as it released his sperm made her come again.

She was still in that languid pleasure state of hazed fulfilment when he moved away and the other two workmen took possession of her body.

Bianca was moved from the table and stood between them as they pulled at her flesh, twisting her breasts, filling their hands with the softness of her buttocks, fingers digging inside her vagina.

They kissed her, one on her mouth, one at her neck or a breast, their trousers pushed down around their thighs and their naked pricks rubbing against her thighs and buttocks. After minutes of this unplanned feeling and rubbing, the blond leaned back against the table and pushed Bianca's head down towards his groin.

She went willingly, bending from the waist as the evil one held her by the hips from behind. The prick went into her mouth and she knew from the quiver of the man's stomach that he would not last long. She sucked, licked and rubbed it against her face, her fingers working the base and raising his pleasure.

Behind her, the evil one pushed his erection into

her vagina. He fucked her for a short time but the giant had made the path too easy and he withdrew and found a different entrance that he first moistened with the juices from her groove.

His finger went in and she squirmed at the sensation and he grunted and guided his prick into her anus. She let him all the way in and then held him tight, contracting the tight hole around his member before squirming again. He yelled at the sensation.

The evil one came, and his violent movements against her buttocks, combined with the heady effects of her fellation, also brought the blond to a climax but, as both men shook and Bianca also shook with her own orgasm, his prick slipped from her mouth, shooting his sperm into her face.

When they staggered away from her, Bianca did not attempt to wipe the spillage from her features. She let it remain, snailing down a cheek and from her chin to drip onto her breasts.

She rested against the table and stared at the men, demanding with her eyes that they recover swiftly and take her again. Demanding that they prove their manhood.

They did, too, during an hour when they worked through all their fantasies and computations, and when she manoeuvred them into the correct position for all three to enter at the same time, in her mouth, vagina and anus, to the mutual pleasure of them all.

As the time passed, so did the balance of power that had started with the potential for fear as three muscled men had confronted a half-naked young woman. Now, the men began to realise that it was Bianca who was in control and not them and, rather than make demands, they followed directions.

Finally, she had had enough and, she guessed, so had they. She suspected they had achieved their last orgasm mainly through pride. They acknowledged that it was over and, dressed to the waist once more, stood around, unsure of what to do next.

The blond brought her a bottle of water with which to wash herself but Bianca didn't want to clean away the dirt and sweat and sperm that covered her body. She did, however, compromise by wiping her face.

Bianca put on the still clean dress that managed to be both demure and sexual and fastened the bodice. She would carry the excesses of the encounter upon her body back to the hotel hidden beneath its respectability.

The giant awkwardly put his hand in his pocket and took out a crumpled banknote which he put on the table. He gave his companions meaningful looks and they, too, put money on the table.

Bianca smiled and spread the notes. The amount was small but probably counted for a lot to the three men. From her handbag, she took her wallet and removed three notes of large denomination.

She placed the notes on the table, smiled sweetly at her working-class lovers, and said: '*Merci.*'

They did not say anything as she left but remained silent in the room, the sunlight from the mouth of God in the wall, spotlighting the cash with which they had been paid for their services.

Her body ached with fulfilment and her mind was clean and free and she belonged to nobody but herself.

Bianca walked down the street towards the taxi rank at the metro station with a new commitment to life: to enjoy.